THE 21ST JUROR

BY FREDERICK CAMPBELL

First Edition 2025

Publisher: MK Storyworks
Cover and Interior Design: MK Storyworks
Author: Frederick Campbell

ISBN: 978-1-80700-038-7

TABLE OF CONTENTS

ABOUT THE AUTHOR

Frederick Campbell lives in the serene, historic city of Charleston, South Carolina, where the quiet beauty of the low country provides a sharp contrast to the high-intensity worlds of political and legal suspense he creates.

A lifelong observer of institutional power, Campbell specializes in thrillers and non-fiction works that explore the intersection of law, finance, and global intelligence. His work focuses on the compromised institutions—the quiet levers of power—and the exceptional individuals forced to operate outside established systems to save them.

When not writing, Campbell consults discreetly on matters of judicial integrity and international asset retrieval, often drawing on this experience to lend authenticity to his novels.

You can follow his journey and find updates on the next book through his publisher, MK Storyworks

DEDICATION

To the relentless pursuit of truth, even when the law demands silence.

And to every person who has ever had to break the rules to fix the system.

PART I

THE SUMMONS

CHAPTER 1

The Call (Charlotte Reed)

18:12—Manhattan Federal Courthouse

The clock above the carved mahogany wall read six twelve. For Charlotte Reed, time was currency, and she had just invested eighteen grueling months into a single moment.

"In the matter of *United States v. OmniCorp*," the clerk announced, his voice booming like a final judgment, "has the jury reached a verdict?"

A murmur rippled through the packed gallery. Charlotte stood beside her client, Robert Wexler, whose sweaty palm was gripping her silk sleeve. Wexler, the CEO of a multi-billion dollar tech firm, was facing decades for corporate espionage. He was guilty. Charlotte knew it. But guilt was an emotion; the law dealt only in evidence. And Charlotte had methodically dismantled the prosecution's evidence, piece by painstaking piece, during a closing argument that had lasted five hours and used zero notes.

The jury foreman, a woman with piercing, skeptical eyes, stood.

"We have, Your Honor."

Judge Alcott took the folded slip. The pause, Charlotte knew, was the most critical tool in any trial lawyer's arsenal. She had used it to great effect yesterday, allowing the silence to drown the jury in the weight of reasonable doubt. The Judge used it now, stretching the tension until the air felt brittle.

He handed the slip back to the clerk.

The clerk's voice rang out, clear and final: "On the charge of Conspiracy to Commit Espionage, we find the defendant, Robert Wexler…"

Not Guilty.

The words weren't even fully formed when Wexler collapsed onto the defense table with a sob of relief.

Charlotte didn't flinch. She simply nodded once to the jury, collected her papers with clinical precision, and allowed a faint, satisfied smile to touch her lips. Perfect record maintained.

She turned toward the door, already mentally moving on to the next case, the next battlefield. Her secured phone, nestled deep in her briefcase, began to vibrate with a specific, encrypted pattern reserved for only one person.

She slipped into the quiet, carpeted hallway before answering.

"Wilfred," she said, her voice crisp.

The voice on the other end, that of her senior partner, Wilfred Sinclair, was usually calm, possessing a soothing baritone that settled multi-million dollar deals. Now, it was strained, the voice of a man who'd just seen a ghost.

"Drop everything, Charlotte. Right now. You need to be on the D.C. shuttle in forty minutes. I have an unprecedented situation."

"Unprecedented? Wilfred, I just finished the trial of the year. I'm scheduled for a victory dinner—"

"This makes OmniCorp look like a parking ticket," Wilfred cut in, his words clipped and urgent. "We just got the call from his Chief of Staff. It's Senator Marcus David Gray."

Charlotte stopped walking. *Gray.* The magnetic, untouchable frontrunner for the Presidency.

"What about him?"

A beat of absolute silence hummed over the encrypted line.

Then, Wilfred delivered the chilling, necessary blow.

"They found Sarah Jenkins dead. And the police are already waiting for him at the townhome."

CHAPTER 2

The Residence (Detective Anne Austin)

21:55—Georgetown Townhome, Washington D.C.

Detective Anne Austin paused at the threshold of the master bedroom, her eyes moving methodically from left to right, cataloging the scene before any photographer entered. She wasn't driven by media hype or political pressure; she was driven by the cold, immutable science of the scene.

Senator Marcus David Gray's Georgetown residence was sleek, modern, and insulated against the outside world. It was also, Anne noted immediately, too clean for a murder.

The victim, Sarah Jenkins, was sprawled across the plush, white rug at the foot of the king-sized bed. Her clothes were disheveled, her throat bore distinct ligature marks, and her striking green eyes were fixed in an empty stare toward the ceiling. The cause of death was clear.

But Anne wasn't looking at the victim. She was looking at the details that spoke of intent.

On the nightstand, beside an untouched carafe of iced water and a stack of policy briefs, sat the Senator's reading glasses and a copy of *The Federalist Papers.* Everything was perfectly aligned, suggesting a serene end to a long day of work.

It was the slippers that caught her attention.

The victim's bedroom slippers—a pair of simple, white terry cloth slides—were lying precisely six feet from the body, tucked neatly against the wall of the walk-in closet. The distance itself wasn't odd, but the manner in which they lay was: they were side-by-side, toes pointing toward the closet, suggesting they had been placed there, not kicked off in a frantic struggle for life.

Anne knelt by the slippers, snapping a discreet photo with her work phone. If the victim was engaged in a violent struggle, her last moments characterized by panic and resistance, her shoes would be scattered, perhaps caught beneath the body or tossed wildly.

Staged, Anne wrote mentally. The scene was arranged to look like a sudden, passionate eruption of violence between two intimate partners, exactly the kind of crime Senator Gray's defense team would struggle to fight. But the quiet order of the room suggested a cold, deliberate choreography.

A uniformed officer approached, holding an evidence bag. "Detective Austin, Senator Gray's phone. Retrieved from the downstairs study. Locked."

"Secure it, tag it, and get a warrant request to Judge Lomax immediately," Anne instructed, her eyes still tracing the subtle, almost invisible scuff mark on the hardwood floor near the closet door—the specific mark she had flagged in her earlier mental assessment. It was an abrasion that was too deep for a slipper, too wide for a leather shoe, and strangely angled. It didn't belong to the Senator, the victim, or any routine furniture move.

Just then, her phone buzzed. It was Georgia Wright, the Assistant District Attorney, already pressing hard.

"Austin, it's Georgia. I need that initial report now. And I mean *now*. The press is setting up outside the perimeter. We need to control the narrative."

"The narrative is secondary to the facts, Ms. Wright. The initial report will be on your desk in two hours, after the forensics team finishes mapping. We have a set of anomalies here that suggest this wasn't quite what it looks like."

"Anomalies?" Georgia's voice sharpened. "What anomalies?"

"Nothing definitive yet," Anne said, deliberately vague. "Just a sense that someone cleaned up too well. And I need a secondary search warrant for the residence next door. Townhome number 21. Just a hunch."

"Townhome 21? Why? Don't get cute, Anne. Stick to the man who was in the room. This case is simple, high-profile, and politically explosive. Don't complicate it."

Anne ended the call. She looked back at the slippers, then at the deep, strange scuff mark. The political machine was already grinding, demanding a simple answer. Anne Austin was already looking for the complex truth.

CHAPTER 3

The Offer (Charlotte Reed)

23:40—White House Complex Annex, Washington D.C.

The meeting was not held in a secure government building, nor in the opulent offices of the Gray campaign. It was in a bunker, a rented, sterile conference room on the tenth floor of a forgotten federal annex building near Foggy Bottom, chosen for its anonymity and shielded lines. The room smelled of new carpet and stale coffee, a stark contrast to the gravity of the men waiting inside.

Charlotte Reed entered, her expensive, navy suit crisp despite the rapid flight from New York. She carried the energy of a storm front, moving quickly but with precise control. She did not look tired; she looked dangerous.

Wilfred Sinclair and Rupert McCallister rose immediately. Wilfred, her partner, looked haggard, his typically impeccable tie slightly askew, his dark eyes shadowed with genuine fear. Rupert McCallister, the barrister brought in for his renowned courtroom spectacle, looked merely irritated by the late hour, adjusting the cuff of his bespoke suit with detached grace.

But all light and focus in the room were drawn to the man seated at the head of the long mahogany table: Senator Marcus David Gray.

The Senator was exactly as he appeared on television: handsome, prematurely graying at the temples, possessing a jawline that belonged on a bust in the Capitol, and an air of unflappable, benevolent authority. He was dressed in tailored slacks and a white dress shirt, open at the collar. He looked tired, yes, but not terrified. He looked, Charlotte observed, deeply inconvenienced.

"Charlotte, thank you for coming so quickly," Wilfred said, his voice low.

"Mr. Sinclair," Charlotte returned, her gaze fixed on the Senator. She ignored the offered hand from Rupert and moved to the empty chair directly across from Gray. She didn't sit immediately; she used her height and posture to dominate the space.

"Senator," she said, her voice cutting through the silence, "I understand you require representation for a matter that has escalated beyond mere political damage control."

Marcus David Gray offered a practiced, rueful smile. "Ms. Reed. I've followed your career. The OmniCorp verdict was masterful. I need a master now." He gestured to the empty chair. "Please. Sit."

Charlotte finally took the seat. She opened her briefcase, retrieving a pristine yellow legal pad and a pen, but she didn't touch them. She let her posture and her silence do the talking.

"Before we discuss retainers, strategy, or even the basic facts of the case, Senator," Charlotte began, her eyes unwavering, "we discuss the absolute truth. I have zero tolerance for surprises, half-truths, or tactical omissions. If I am to save your life—and make no mistake, that is the literal stakes of a murder charge against a figure like you—you must be an open book. Any lie you tell me now is a lie that will destroy us in court. So, tell me the single, most critical fact: Did you kill Sarah Jenkins?"

The question was delivered without inflection, without judgment. It was purely transactional.

Gray held her gaze for a full five seconds. His expression didn't crack. It was a performance, but one delivered with such sincere belief that Charlotte's professional alarm bells began to chime.

"I did not kill Sarah," Gray stated firmly, leaning forward slightly, invoking the confidentiality of the room. "I loved Sarah. She was my Chief of Staff, my campaign manager, and yes, for the last year, my most trusted confidante and, regrettably, my lover. But I did not lay a hand on her. That entire scene—her death, the police being called—is a vicious, politically motivated attack designed to sink my campaign and my life."

Wilfred cleared his throat nervously. "We have instructed the Senator to maintain radio silence on the relationship for now, Charlotte. It's inflammatory."

"I don't care about inflammation, Wilfred," Charlotte snapped, not looking at him. "I care about the prosecution's narrative. Senator, you were the last person known to be in the residence. Detective Austin has confirmed your DNA is under her fingernails. Explain that. Don't give me a campaign speech."

Gray sighed, running a manicured hand over his weary face. "We had an argument. A terrible one. It was late. She was passionate about an issue—a deep disagreement over foreign policy direction—and she wanted me to publicly reverse a key stance. I refused. Things got heated. There was some shouting.

She grabbed my arm, hard. I pulled away. I left the room, went down to my study, and worked until three AM. I returned to the bedroom around four. She was dead.”

“And the argument involved her grabbing your arm forcefully enough to transfer your DNA under her nail, but not enough for you to require medical attention?” Charlotte pressed. “That’s convenient.”

“It’s the truth,” Gray insisted. “It was a struggle of wills. I was pushing her away. I had no idea about her death until the morning.”

Charlotte stared at the Senator, calculating. Gray was capable of lying on policy, capable of lying to the electorate, capable of lying to his wife. But lying to the lawyer who held his freedom in her hand? That required a specific kind of arrogance. He was hiding something, but was it the murder? Or was it something far more complex?

Charlotte knew about secrets. She used them, she exploited them, and she occasionally buried her own. She thought, briefly, of the early days of her career, the case of the environmental activist she’d defended who was clearly guilty of sabotage. She had successfully argued self-defense based on a manufactured psychological profile. The case had launched her career, given her the perfect record she now guarded fiercely. But the compromise—the knowledge that she had knowingly freed a dangerous man—had left a residue of moral rot she masked with perfection.

She stood again, pushing her chair back slightly. The subtle movement broke the tension, forcing everyone else to look up at her.

“Senator Gray, I don’t believe you,” Charlotte said flatly.

Wilfred’s eyes went wide. Rupert McCallister actually made a low, guttural noise of shock. Gray, however, remained composed, only the slightest tightening around his eyes betraying his frustration.

"I'm not calling you a murderer. I'm saying you are not telling me the whole story," Charlotte clarified, pacing slowly behind her chair. "The scene is too tidy. Your timeline is too neat. And the fact that the police were called so quickly and the prosecution is moving with this kind of lightning political speed suggests a setup. If it's a setup, the key to your defense is not denying the argument; it's finding the conspirator. And to do that, I need to know every single person Sarah Jenkins was talking to, what she was arguing about *before* your late-night confrontation, and every single financial dealing she managed for you, no matter how small or off-the-books."

She stopped, leaning her knuckles on the table. "Frankly, Senator, my gut tells me you are telling a legal lie of omission. You didn't kill her, but you know who did, or you know the secret she died protecting. And if you continue to protect that secret, you'll be the next occupant of a federal prison cell."

"My secret is my campaign, Ms. Reed," Gray said, his voice finally showing a touch of steel. "I am a Presidential candidate. Every secret I have is political."

"Then let's talk terms," Charlotte said, changing tack, deciding in that moment she would walk away unless the offer was worth the total demolition of her life for the next year. "My retainer for a case of this magnitude, which will absorb my full focus and require the relocation of my entire team to Washington D.C., is eight million dollars, paid in full, non-refundable, before I file a single notice of appearance. My hourly rate thereafter is three thousand dollars. Do not insult me by attempting to negotiate. That is the price for a perfect defense."

Silence descended, heavy and thick. The sum was astronomical, even for a candidate funded by major political action committees.

Gray looked at Wilfred, a silent question passing between them. Wilfred looked panicked, shaking his head slightly—the number was too high, even for the campaign's 'black budget.'

As Gray prepared to object or counter-offer, Wilfred Sinclair moved. It was a movement only Charlotte noticed, practiced and almost invisible. He reached into his leather binder and, while pretending to review a legal document for Rupert, he subtly slid a thin, folded piece of paper beneath Charlotte's yellow legal pad.

Charlotte glanced down, casually placing her hand over the pad. The paper was not campaign stationery. It was a printout from a secure ledger, deliberately photocopied badly to look like trash.

She barely spared it a millisecond of sight, but what she saw was enough.

The document was a Wire Transfer Confirmation. It detailed a disbursement of $450,000 made three weeks ago. The recipient was labeled only as a numbered account, but the sender was explicitly identified as Sarah Jenkins. The memo line, however, had been manually highlighted in neon yellow marker: *Payment for Services Rendered – 21 Holdings LLC.*

Charlotte instantly recognized the name: 21 Holdings LLC. It was a shell company the FBI had been tracking for years, rumored to be a ghost front for offshore political influence, but one that always disappeared before it could be tied to a specific politician. Furthermore, the number 21 was a staggering coincidence, recalling Detective Austin's early, unconfirmed suspicions about the townhome next door.

But the most damning detail was the address of the recipient bank: Belgrade, Serbia. This wasn't local political corruption. This was a sophisticated, transnational operation involving vast sums of unaccounted money being moved through a known shell corporation—a shell corporation that the murdered Chief of Staff was *paying*.

This was not a murder cover-up for a failed affair. This was a murder cover-up for a shadow political network attempting to buy the Presidency.

Charlotte's gaze lifted from the paper and locked back onto Senator Gray. His face was still a mask of composed innocence regarding the murder, but now, Charlotte saw the deep, calculating fear in his eyes. He wasn't afraid of the jury; he was afraid of what the investigation would uncover about his finances. Sarah Jenkins hadn't been murdered over a policy spat; she had been murdered because she was trying to wire the Senator's foreign handlers a massive payoff or, conversely, expose the fact that she was the one handling the foreign wires and got caught.

The entire landscape of the case shifted, transforming from a simple criminal defense into a chess game against unseen global powers. The risk, the stakes, and the complexity had just multiplied tenfold.

Charlotte finally sat down, placing her pen deliberately on the legal pad, resting it precisely over the highlighted Serbian transaction. The eight million dollars now seemed trivial. She had to take this case. Not for the money, or the record, but for the sheer, terrifying challenge of it.

"The eight million is acceptable, Senator," Charlotte said, her voice now colder than ever.

Gray's face broke into a relieved, practiced smile. "Excellent. Welcome to the team, Ms. Reed. I assure you, we will win."

"No," Charlotte corrected him, leaning forward until the distance between them felt electric. "*I* will win. But we are going to do this my way. Rupert, Wilfred, you are now under my direct command. Senator, your press team is fired. Your wife and children are off limits to the media. You speak only to me. And we are going to start by pulling every single shred of financial data related to Sarah Jenkins' personal and campaign accounts for the last six months. Everything. The political fallout is now secondary to the truth. Do you understand your instructions?"

Gray nodded slowly, the presidential veneer momentarily stripped away, revealing the desperate client beneath. "Perfectly, Charlotte. What is our first move?"

Charlotte stood, slipping the damning wire transfer slip into a hidden compartment in her briefcase. "Our first move is to file a motion to dismiss based on prejudicial charging by the ADA, followed by a demand for expedited discovery. We attack the prosecution's timeline before they even finalize the indictment. We do not defend; we go on the offense. And we will find out exactly who tried to frame you, Senator. Or, more accurately, who arranged for this convenient distraction."

As she walked toward the door, leaving the three men to process the strategic shift, she glanced back at Wilfred Sinclair. He gave her a subtle, almost imperceptible nod. He had wanted her to see the financial truth, the truth that transcended the murder. He had set her on the path. The perfect legal lie—the omission that forced her to take the case—had been executed flawlessly.

Charlotte stepped into the hallway, pulling her phone from her pocket. The time was just after midnight. She typed a quick, encrypted message to her lead paralegal back in New York.

Initiate deep dive on 21 Holdings LLC. All ties to Belgrade, any political figures, and Judge Joseph Lomax. Priorities shifted. Tell no one.

The game was no longer about a murder. It was about a shadow government, and Charlotte Reed had just accepted the contract to dismantle it.

CHAPTER 4

The 21st Door (Detective Anne Austin)

01:30—Georgetown Townhome District, D.C.

The cold seeped into Anne Austin's bones, but it wasn't the January air. It was the icy spike of adrenaline that came from the anonymous text message she'd received less than an hour ago.

The text was still open on her secured phone, the screen dimmed against the night: a blurred photo of her own apartment building's entrance, taken from an unusual high angle, followed by three stark words: *Ask about the 21st.*

The threat was unambiguous: *We know where you live. Back off.*

But the threat contained a clue, and Anne was a detective, trained to treat every piece of information, no matter how menacing, as evidence. The number 21 flashed in her mind. Townhome 21. The address immediately adjacent to Senator Gray's property—the same property she had instinctively requested a warrant for, only to have her request sharply denied by Georgia Wright, the ADA, who insisted the focus must remain squarely on the Senator.

Anne sat in her unmarked Chevy, parked six blocks from the Gray residence. The street was quiet now, the patrol cars having dispersed, leaving only a thin yellow line of crime scene tape fluttering weakly in the breeze. She had filed her initial reports, confirming the time of death and the DNA transfer, giving the prosecution exactly what they wanted: the clean, simple narrative of a powerful man in a rage. But she had deliberately omitted her hunch about the slippers and the strange, non-committal scuff mark.

She pulled the case file's perimeter surveillance log up on her tablet. The Gray townhomes were part of a block of three identical, highly secured luxury units. Gray occupied the middle one. The one to the left was empty, awaiting a multi-million dollar sale. The one to the right was Townhome 21.

The security cameras covering Gray's entrance, which Anne had reviewed earlier, showed nothing suspicious—no cars, no loiterers, just the intermittent shadow of a patrol officer. But the log also included a single, throwaway notation from a private security guard's patrol report at 04:15 a.m., roughly fifteen minutes after Gray claimed to have discovered the body: *Minor noise complaint at 21. Investigated. Nothing observed. Possible HVAC unit.*

Anne re-read the entry three times. A "noise complaint" at 04:15 a.m., just as the medical examiner's preliminary estimate placed Sarah Jenkins' death, which was supposed to be a quiet, private strangulation. This was not a coincidence. This was the signal. Someone was leaving a trail.

She reached for the secure radio, then stopped. Calling in a new lead—especially one based on an anonymous threat and a "feeling" about a staged crime scene—would lead to immediate interference from Georgia Wright's office, likely backed by the political clout of Judge Joseph Lomax, who was clearly already involved in the D.C. political circuit (as indicated by the "J.L." flagged in the text messages).

If I call it in, I get shut down. If I go alone, I'm trespassing.

Anne made her decision, driven by the cold fear of the threat and the professional imperative to solve the case, not just close the file. She had to breach Townhome 21 now, before the noise complaint entry was redacted, the logs were scrubbed, or the true occupant of the home realized the number *21* had been flagged.

She radioed dispatch with a cover story: "Routine perimeter check. Gray residence. Advise all units I'll be off-mic for thirty minutes investigating a possible electrical trip on the adjacent exterior perimeter. Standard precaution."

She parked her car, grabbed her tactical kit—gloves, flashlight, and a small, state-of-the-art lock-picking kit she hadn't needed since her undercover days—and slipped into the shadows of the alley running between Gray's home and Townhome 21.

The alley was narrow, smelling of refuse and damp concrete. A single, high-mounted exterior light provided poor illumination. Anne moved with the silence of a predator, pressing herself against the brickwork. She reached the back entrance of Townhome 21. The door was steel, equipped with a high-security electronic keypad. Too clean, too new.

She pulled out her lock-picking kit. Years of training kicked in, the subtle language of tumblers and springs. She didn't have time for a full bypass. She needed a quick, brute-force entry without setting off a silent alarm. She found the small, almost invisible maintenance panel beneath the keypad—a known weakness in this particular model of security system. She worked swiftly, bypassing the primary power source and creating a temporary surge, causing the keypad's lights to flicker once, then die. The door clicked open.

Amateur hour, Anne thought, stepping inside. *No one uses this system without modifying the maintenance bypass.*

The interior of Townhome 21 was the polar opposite of Senator Gray's modern, personalized space. It was clinical, Spartan, and devoid of personality. The main room was empty save for a low table, two utilitarian chairs, and a large, empty rack bolted to the wall where a high-definition monitor had clearly been removed very recently. The air was cold, stale, and bore the faint, metallic scent of ozone, the kind of smell left behind by powerful, continuously running electronic equipment.

Anne's flashlight beam danced across the walls. There were no pictures, no personal items, and no signs of Sarah Jenkins or Marcus David Gray ever having been here. This was not a second residence; it was an operations base.

She moved to the window facing Gray's residence—the window directly overlooking the side of the master bedroom suite where Sarah Jenkins had been found. The glass was polarized, perfectly tinted to allow someone inside to observe the Senator's room without being seen. On the windowsill, Anne found a single, small brass casing—the kind used for a high-powered, directional microphone.

"You son of a…" Anne whispered. It was a surveillance outpost. Someone hadn't just watched Senator Gray; they had been monitoring him, perhaps recording him, and were in the perfect position to witness—or execute—the crime next door.

She moved quickly through the rest of the silent townhome. The kitchen was unused. The bathroom held a single toothbrush and a generic, disposable razor. Upstairs, the master bedroom was just as bare. The only evidence she found was in the walk-in closet, behind a false panel in the wall.

Anne pulled the panel open. Inside was a small, waterproof duffel bag. She unzipped it, revealing not clothes, but a single, custom-made silencer wrapped in an oil cloth, and a micro-SD card sealed in an anti-static pouch. The silencer was pristine, clearly never fired, suggesting the murder weapon was a different instrument, or still at large.

The SD card was the prize. This contained the surveillance data, the recordings, the true timeline. This was the proof she needed to turn the entire case sideways.

Anne pocketed the silencer and the SD card, her heart pounding a heavy rhythm against her ribs. She was alone, in an unsecured location, possessing highly sensitive evidence linking the murder to a shadow operation. She had to get out, secure the evidence, and find a way to analyze the card without alerting Georgia Wright or the Judge.

She moved back downstairs toward the front door, planning to reset the maintenance bypass and disappear into the night.

Just as her hand reached for the dead-bolt, the heavy steel door was violently wrenched inward.

Anne stumbled back, momentarily blinded by the sudden surge of light from the outside and the massive silhouette filling the doorway.

The man was over six feet tall, broad-shouldered, and wearing a black, featureless tactical vest. His face was covered by a dark cloth mask, leaving only his eyes visible—cold, professional, and entirely focused on her.

Anne didn't hesitate. She threw her flashlight, aiming for his head. The man grunted but barely flinched, charging across the threshold.

"Drop the bag!" the masked man commanded, his voice muffled but low and guttural. He was not a thief. He was an operative.

Anne scrambled backward, drawing the small, standard-issue .38 she carried in a shoulder holster. She leveled the weapon, her finger already on the trigger. "Police! Drop your weapon!"

The operative ignored the command. He didn't draw a weapon; he simply moved, fast and low, executing a practiced, disarming technique. He kicked the small table, sending it spinning into Anne's legs, throwing her balance off.

Before she could recover, he was on her.

The next few seconds were a blur of violent, professional struggle. Anne fought with the brutal intensity of someone fighting for their life. She managed to land an elbow into his ribs, eliciting a sharp gasp of pain, but the man's size and training were overwhelming. He grabbed her wrist, twisting the gun from her grasp with a sickening crunch of bone, sending the .38 skittering across the hardwood floor.

Then, with frightening efficiency, he slammed her back against the wall, pinning her throat with his forearm. The lack of air was immediate and absolute.

Anne clawed desperately at his arm, her vision tunneling to a gray-red haze. She could hear the blood roaring in her ears, drowning out the frantic, silent scream trapped in her chest.

"Where is the card?" the operative hissed, his voice close to her ear. "The SD card. Where did you put it?"

He knew. He hadn't come for a random search. He had come for the evidence she had just secured.

In a last, desperate move, as her lungs burned and her consciousness frayed, Anne managed to hook her foot around the discarded table leg and pull.

The table came crashing down onto the man's leg. He cried out in surprise and pain, momentarily releasing the pressure on her throat.

Anne fell to the floor, coughing violently, gasping for life-giving air. The operative was momentarily stunned, looking down at his injured leg.

It was enough time.

Anne rolled, not toward her discarded gun, but toward the open door. She scrambled out into the cold alleyway, ignoring the burning agony in her wrist. The operative yelled, struggling to follow.

She ran, using the zig-zagging geometry of the Georgetown alleys, forcing the larger man to maneuver through tight spaces. She didn't stop until she reached the relative safety of the main avenue, melting into the shadows of a vacant storefront.

She leaned against the cold glass, struggling to breathe, the pain in her wrist now registering as a deep, throbbing agony. She was bruised, likely concussed, and terrified, but she was alive.

More importantly, she felt the slight, hard square object still nestled in her pocket. The SD card. She had been disarmed, almost killed, but she had secured the evidence.

She pulled out her work phone, dialing a number she hadn't called in years—a former FBI contact in the cybercrimes unit she knew hated political interference as much as she did. She didn't dare call the D.C. police, not now, knowing what she knew about Judge Joseph Lomax and the political reach of the network.

"This is Austin," she rasped, her voice rough from the strangulation. "I need a meet. Now. Secure access only. I have a digital file that links the Gray murder to a transnational network, and I just got jumped by a professional hitman at Townhome 21."

She looked back toward the dark alley, the only witness to the violence. She had the evidence that could clear a presidential candidate or expose a deep state threat, and she was running for her life. The clock was ticking, and the game had just turned deadly.

CHAPTER 5

The Bench Warning (Charlotte Reed)

08:00—Defense Command Center, D.C.

Charlotte Reed walked back into the sterile conference room in the federal annex. Dawn was gray and cold over Washington, but inside, the air was hot with tension. Senator Gray, looking rumpled but still presidential, was engaged in a hushed, nervous conversation with Rupert McCallister. Wilfred Sinclair, however, was nowhere to be seen.

"Where is Wilfred?" Charlotte demanded, dropping her briefcase onto the mahogany table.

Rupert looked up, annoyed at the interruption. "Sinclair? He had an emergency. Said something about a necessary family diversion. He left a message with the security guard that he'd be out of pocket indefinitely. Most unprofessional timing, if you ask me."

Charlotte felt a cold, professional dread. *Unnecessary family diversion.* That was the first lie. Wilfred Sinclair had no family he cared about more than his reputation, and that was second only to his control. She knew instinctively he hadn't left for a family emergency; he had fled. And his departure was linked directly to the cryptic wire transfer he had forced her to see hours earlier.

She walked immediately to the spot where she had been sitting the previous night. Her yellow legal pad was still there, pen resting neatly across the top. She lifted the pad, and there it was: a small, cream-colored note, folded twice, placed exactly where the Belgrade wire transfer slip had been.

It was handwritten on thick, expensive paper—Wilfred's personal stationery—but the handwriting was deliberately rushed, almost illegible. She unfolded it.

Don't trust the Bench.

The three words hit her with the force of a physical blow. *The Bench.* It didn't mean the D.C. court system generally. It meant one man: Judge Joseph Lomax.

Charlotte's mind flashed back to the message she had encrypted and sent to her lead paralegal: *Initiate deep dive on 21 Holdings LLC. All ties to Belgrade, any political figures, and Judge Joseph Lomax.* Wilfred had confirmed the massive scope of the operation, given her the critical financial thread, and now, he had vanished, leaving a direct warning about the one person who could unilaterally dismiss the case or ensure Gray's conviction.

"What is that?" Rupert asked, stepping closer, drawn by the sudden rigidity in Charlotte's posture.

Charlotte crumpled the note instantly, slipping it into the inner pocket of her suit jacket. "Nothing. Just a note about a canceled appointment. Wilfred is officially a liability, Rupert. You and I run point now. No one, and I mean no one, is to be told about his absence. We frame this as him handling the financial logistics out of a secure, remote location."

Rupert huffed, clearly displeased but compliant. "Very well. What are the logistics? We have the pre-trial hearing for the prosecution's motion to compel discovery at eleven. Georgia Wright will use this hearing to demand Senator Gray's full financial disclosure dating back ten years, citing the alleged political motivation for the murder."

"Let her," Charlotte said, the chilling calm returning to her voice. She pulled out her phone. It was time for the first report from her New York team.

The secure message came through, a dense three-page summary from her paralegal, Ben, detailing the initial findings on the shell company. Charlotte skimmed the text, absorbing the complex, damning information in seconds.

21 Holdings LLC, The Belgrade Connection.

- Establishment: 21 Holdings was established 18 months ago in the Cayman Islands, quickly establishing a small, non-descript office in a business park in Belgrade, Serbia.
- Funding Source: Initial funding, over $30 million, came from a series of untraceable "bearer shares" purchased through two separate holding companies, both linked to known Russian oligarchs with ties to state intelligence agencies. The money was routed through Cyprus, Malta, and then finally to Belgrade. This wasn't organized crime; this was statecraft.
- The Gray Link: The $450,000 payment from Sarah Jenkins (Gray's victim and Chief of Staff) was the only transaction *outgoing* from a U.S.-based entity. All other funds flowed *into* the organization. The transaction memo—*Payment for Services Rendered*—was professional cover. Ben's analysis concluded that Sarah Jenkins wasn't paying *for* a service; she was paying *into*

the operation, possibly as an agent, or as a blackmail victim paying tribute.

- The Judge: The initial cross-reference on Judge Joseph Lomax was chillingly sparse. He had no direct financial ties to 21 Holdings, but Ben found a single, archived photo from a deep-access political blog: a blurry image of Judge Lomax shaking hands with a known intermediary for the Russian oligarch who founded the shell companies, taken six months ago at a private, unlisted D.C. policy conference. The caption simply read: *Lomax and the Policy King.*

The sheer audacity of the operation took Charlotte's breath away. Senator Gray was either the knowing puppet or the unwitting face of an operation designed to place a foreign asset in the White House. Sarah Jenkins was the treasurer or the traitor. And Judge Joseph Lomax, the man presiding over the murder trial, was, at the very least, professionally acquainted with the people funding the entire conspiracy.

Don't trust the Bench. Wilfred's warning was now a terrifying certainty.

"Alright, Rupert," Charlotte said, slamming the phone shut. "Here is the revised strategy. We don't just fight Georgia Wright's motion to compel. We preempt it, and we hit them with a sledgehammer."

Rupert leaned in, his expression finally alight with interest. "The counter-offensive. I like it. But on what grounds? We can't reveal the financial tie to Serbia yet; we need more time to trace the actual purpose of that $450,000."

"We attack the process, not the substance," Charlotte explained, pacing. "We file an emergency counter-motion immediately: Motion for Expedited and Prejudicial Discovery of Prosecutorial Misconduct and Judicial Impropriety."

Rupert frowned. "Impropriety? That's highly inflammatory, Charlotte. You can't accuse a sitting Federal Judge of impropriety without smoking gun evidence, or you risk sanctions that will bury us."

"We won't accuse; we'll suggest," Charlotte countered, her voice dropping to a conspiratorial whisper. "We use the one piece of evidence the Judge allowed us to see last night: the communication logs between the prosecution and the Lead Investigator. We argue that the speed and focus of the charging decision—ignoring all leads that point away from the Senator—suggests a political motivation. We then use the 'J.L.' text flag, which you may recall we pulled from those logs, as evidence of a pre-existing, undisclosed relationship between the ADA and the presiding Judge."

"You mean the text about the 'J.L. confirmed for the 15th' fundraiser?" Rupert scoffed. "That's flimsy. It could be any J.L."

"Perhaps," Charlotte agreed, meeting his cynicism with cold logic. "But when the stakes are the Presidency, any appearance of impropriety is fatal. We don't need to prove they are corrupt. We only need to force Judge Lomax to rule on a motion that demands the discovery of his *own* private communications with the ADA. He will either recuse himself, or he will deny the motion, confirming our suspicion of bias and giving us an immediate, massive appealable error."

Rupert McCallister smiled slowly, a genuine, appreciative look replacing his irritation. "My God, Charlotte. You're brilliant. You're asking the Judge to stab himself with his own gavel. If he allows discovery of his own communications, the case against Gray is tainted by the appearance of a fix. If he denies it, he gives us the grounds for a mistrial or a change of venue. Either way, we stop the indictment process cold."

Charlotte nodded. "We need the time that buying a successful motion provides. Time to figure out what Wilfred was running from, and time for my team to trace the flow of that Serbian money. Time to find the connection between 21 Holdings and the townhome next door."

She sent the fully drafted motion—a document of razor-sharp legal aggression she had worked on through the night—to Rupert for final filing. The filing immediately set the hearing for an emergency motion before Judge Lomax at four that afternoon. The battlefield had been set.

16:00—District Courtroom 302, D.C.

Courtroom 302 was packed, humming with the contained energy of journalists, political aides, and legal observers. The proceedings were technical, but the stakes—the fate of a presidential campaign—made every movement, every word, feel volcanic.

Judge Joseph Lomax sat high above the room, an imposing figure with a solemn face that masked any hint of the man who attended policy conferences with Russian oligarchs' intermediaries. He surveyed the courtroom with the practiced neutrality of someone who knew he was being watched by the world.

"The Court is in receipt of the State's Motion to Compel discovery of Senator Gray's full personal and campaign finances," Judge Lomax announced, his voice deep and resonant. "And, concurrently, we are in receipt of an Emergency Counter-Motion from the Defense: Motion for Expedited and Prejudicial Discovery of Prosecutorial Misconduct and Judicial Impropriety. Ms. Wright, we'll hear your argument first."

Georgia Wright, the ADA, was flawless. She was sharp, concise, and focused solely on the established facts. She argued that the murder of Sarah Jenkins, the Chief of Staff, was undeniably linked to Senator Gray's financial and political pressures, making his full financial history germane to motive and opportunity.

"Your Honor," Georgia concluded, her gaze firm, "the Defense's refusal to turn over these records is nothing short of obstruction. If Senator Gray has nothing to hide, he should open his books and allow the jury to see the full, desperate picture of his financial state, which we contend led to a fatal confrontation with his closest confidante."

"Thank you, Ms. Wright," Judge Lomax said smoothly. "Ms. Reed, your response."

Charlotte rose. She looked directly at Judge Lomax. She felt the subtle tremor of Wilfred's note in her jacket pocket—*Don't trust the Bench*—and channeled the fear into pure, icy determination.

"Your Honor, we will not insult the intelligence of this Court by pretending that this is a routine discovery dispute," Charlotte began. "Ms. Wright's motion is a fishing expedition designed to distract from a fundamentally flawed and politically tainted charging decision. We are not resisting discovery; we are demanding *proper* discovery."

She moved closer to the podium. Rupert McCallister sat behind her, already logging every word of the Judge's reaction.

"The State has provided a timeline that is suspiciously neat, based on a crime scene that was, on its face, manufactured to point a specific finger," Charlotte continued, her voice rising slightly. "And the State's zeal to charge Senator Gray has led them to ignore, or deliberately fail to pursue, exculpatory evidence. This is not about murder; it is about political control.”

She then deployed the attack, using the Judge's own ruling from Chapter 3 against him.

“Our emergency counter-motion is based on the limited, unredacted discovery this Court wisely granted us yesterday: the communication logs between the ADA's office and the Lead Investigator, Detective Anne Austin. In reviewing those records, we found highly unusual, time-sensitive, and encrypted communications between the State and outside parties that raised serious questions about the political neutrality of the charging process.”

Charlotte paused, letting the silence draw all attention to the man in the black robe. Judge Lomax remained impassive, his hands resting on the bench, but Charlotte saw the almost infinitesimal tightening of the skin around his knuckles.

“Specifically, Your Honor, we found a coded reference to a party identified only as 'J.L.' tied to an unscheduled policy meeting just prior to the indictment,” Charlotte pressed, her eyes locking onto Lomax. “While we do not accuse this Court of impropriety, the appearance of an undisclosed relationship, or even the perception that the prosecution is coordinating with non-state actors outside of the discovery process, is sufficient to prejudice the entire proceeding.”

Charlotte brought her fist down, not hard, but with absolute conviction, on the podium.

“Therefore, the Defense demands that the State immediately turn over all communications, including private cell phone records, texts, and emails, between Assistant District Attorney Georgia Wright and any individual identified by the initials 'J.L.' for the last six months, and specifically, for the presiding Judge of this case, Judge Joseph Lomax, for the same time period. We demand to know if the Bench itself is compromised. If this Court denies this motion, Your Honor, we will immediately appeal for a change of venue and a mistrial based on explicit judicial bias."

The courtroom erupted. Georgia Wright sprang to her feet, her face a mask of shocked rage.

"Objection, Your Honor! This is scurrilous! It is a defamatory, baseless attack on the integrity of this Court, purely designed to delay and distract! There is no evidence—"

"Your Honor," Charlotte cut in, her voice calm but penetrating. "The evidence is the undisclosed communication, and the only way to prove or disprove our claim of impropriety is through the discovery we seek. If there is nothing to hide, then Ms. Wright's communications—and this Court's—should be willingly disclosed to maintain the sanctity of the trial."

Judge Lomax raised a hand, silencing the room instantly. The air was thick with the weight of the constitutional crisis Charlotte had just engineered. He was trapped. To grant the motion was to open his own private communications to scrutiny, risking the exposure of his ties to the 21 Holdings network. To deny it was to give Charlotte the golden ticket to an immediate, successful appeal and a change of venue, which would allow the new judge to grant the discovery later anyway.

Lomax stared down at Charlotte Reed. He saw not just a lawyer, but a machine of logic and determination. He understood, in that moment, that Wilfred Sinclair had set his partner loose, and she was now an existential threat to the network.

"Counsel," Judge Lomax said, his voice dangerously measured. "The Court finds the defense's motion highly inappropriate and bordering on contempt. However, this Court is committed to the absolute pursuit of justice and the appearance of impartiality."

He paused, adjusting his glasses, his eyes gleaming with cold cunning.

"The Court denies the Defense's motion in its entirety. It is utterly without merit, speculative, and relies on an inference of initials that is too broad to warrant such an unprecedented invasion of privacy."

A small, satisfied flicker crossed Georgia Wright's face. Charlotte, however, didn't react. She had anticipated this.

"However," Lomax continued, his gaze shifting to Georgia Wright, "I find that Ms. Wright's Motion to Compel discovery of Senator Gray's full finances is also denied. The State has failed to present sufficiently specific evidence linking the alleged financial motive to the commission of the crime, rendering the request a punitive fishing expedition. The defense is ordered to turn over only the financial records related to Sarah Jenkins' personal accounts and any campaign expenditures she directly managed in the last six months."

It was a masterstroke of judicial strategy. Lomax had neutralized both sides. He had protected his own communications by denying Charlotte's motion, thereby confirming his bias for the network. But he had also handcuffed Georgia Wright, preventing her from accessing the Senator's *personal* deep financial ties, which Charlotte needed to protect until she could understand the scale of the conspiracy.

Charlotte felt a surge of professional admiration mixed with sheer horror. Lomax wasn't just compromised; he was a brilliant counter-player. He had just confirmed his place as the 21st Juror, actively managing the information flow to protect his co-conspirators.

"The Court is adjourned until the arraignment hearing," Lomax stated, striking his gavel sharply.

As the room emptied, Charlotte walked past the prosecution table. Georgia Wright looked furious about the denial of her motion, but she also looked strangely calculating.

"You're dancing on the edge of contempt, Reed," Georgia hissed quietly as Charlotte passed.

"You're dancing on the edge of a career-ending ethical violation, Wright," Charlotte countered, pausing just long enough to deliver the blow. "And I saw the J.L. text. The next time, I'll find the sender."

Georgia Wright opened her mouth to snap a denial, but before she could speak, she saw a large, imposing figure standing discreetly in the gallery doorway. The man was impeccably dressed and wearing the same tactical watch as the operative Anne Austin had just encountered at Townhome 21. The man gave Georgia a subtle, chilling nod—a signal.

Charlotte didn't see the man, but she saw Georgia Wright's eyes flick past her, and the prosecutor's look of anger instantly dissolved into one of cold, professional fear. Georgia Wright was being watched, managed, and controlled just as closely as Senator Gray.

Charlotte walked out of the courtroom, the adrenaline fading, leaving behind a sharp, terrible certainty. She had just confirmed that the case, the Judge, and the Prosecutor were all compromised. She was alone on a team of three—Wilfred was gone, Rupert was naive, and Gray was the puppet.

She pulled out her phone and sent a one-word text to her New York team.

Accelerate.

The game was no longer a chess match. It was a race against the clock, with a judge running the clock, and the stakes being the fate of the free world.

CHAPTER 6

The Decryption and the Deal (Detective Anne Austin &
Charlotte Reed)

00:15—A Maintenance Tunnel Beneath the Lincoln Memorial, D.C.

Detective Anne Austin leaned against the damp concrete wall, the stench of stagnant water and dust filling her lungs. Her jacket was ripped, her hair was matted with grime, and her right forearm was already swelling to an alarming size, a sickening deep bruise forming from where the operative had wrenched her gun away. She had made it. She was alive, and the SD card was safe.

She was not alone. Sitting opposite her on an overturned plastic bucket was Elias Vance. Elias, once the top cyber-crimes analyst at the FBI's Washington Field Office, now ran a private, high-end security and intelligence firm that occasionally, reluctantly, cleaned up messes too politically toxic for the Bureau to touch. He was thin, wired, dressed in jeans and a fleece jacket, looking less like a hacker and more like a perpetually sleepless college student.

He examined her wrist with a gentle touch that belied his profession. "You're fractured, Anne. At least three bones. You should be in an E.R."

"If I go to an E.R., the operative from Townhome 21 will know I survived," Anne rasped, her throat still burning. She swallowed hard. "He knows I took the card. If he knows I'm alive, he'll know the card is active. They'll sweep the entire D.C. grid for anomalies."

She reached into her pocket, retrieving the tiny micro-SD card sealed in its anti-static pouch, and the silencer wrapped in oil cloth. She slid them across the floor to Elias.

"This is why I'm here," Anne said. "The card holds surveillance data from Townhome 21. That place was a forward operating base pointed directly at Senator Gray's bedroom. The man who nearly killed me was an operative. Not a common thief, not a random killer. He was trained, professional, and he knew exactly what I was after. He was the same man who was observing Georgia Wright in the courtroom, I'm certain of it, or someone in the same unit. This goes deep, Elias. Foreign deep."

Elias, whose expression rarely shifted from detached concentration, looked up at the silencer. "Custom-machined. Not standard issue. Likely Eastern European origin. Expensive. You interrupt one of their clean-up ops, you're making enemies with people who don't care about warrants or jurisdictions."

He then picked up the SD card, holding it delicately with tweezers. He moved over to his open backpack, which contained a complex array of hardware—a small server rack, several high-powered laptops, and a portable Faraday cage.

"This will be high-level encryption," Elias murmured, already connecting the card to a proprietary reader. "Likely military grade, multi-layer obfuscation. If I try to run a standard brute-force, it'll trip a kill-switch and wipe the data instantly. I have to create a virtual environment, mirror the card's internal structure, and crack the key with minimal intrusion."

The next ninety minutes passed in absolute silence, broken only by the rhythmic hum of Elias's custom-built cooling fan and the soft tap of his fingers on the keyboard. Anne monitored their secured, isolated comms channel, running on a redundant satellite line, while trying to ignore the pulsing agony in her arm. She thought of her boss, Georgia Wright, who had dismissed Townhome 21. She thought of Judge Lomax, whose name kept appearing in the margins of the investigation. The official narrative was a lie; the question now was, how large was the canvas of the truth?

Finally, Elias exhaled sharply.

"Got it," he said. "That was aggressive. Tier 4 encryption, likely custom-built for political espionage."

He pulled up a clean, high-definition video file on the screen. The image was perfectly clear, taken from the vantage point of the master bedroom window in Townhome 21, overlooking Senator Gray's suite. It provided a clear, unobstructed view of the foot of the Gray's bed, the white rug, and the doorway.

The timestamp was critical: 03:15 a.m., roughly ten minutes *after* Senator Gray claimed to have left the room following his argument with Sarah Jenkins.

Anne watched, her heart seizing in her chest.

The video showed the bedroom door opening slowly. The masked operative—the same build, the same movements as Anne's attacker—slipped silently into the room. He was wearing gloves and moving with the fluid, practiced ease of someone who knew exactly where to go.

He did not use a lock pick or a crowbar. He used a key. Sarah Jenkins had given the operative access, or someone with access had given him the key.

The operative moved to Sarah Jenkins, who was already lying prone on the rug. The video confirmed what Dr. Mirza's private toxicology report had suggested: she was incapacitated. The operative administered a small, clear dose of liquid to the victim's mouth—the source of the mysterious trace element Dr. Mirza had flagged.

Then, the true horror: the operative produced a thin, metallic wire, strangling Sarah Jenkins with cold, clinical efficiency. It was murder, pure and professional, devoid of the rage and passion that characterized the police's working theory.

The final, damning sequence was the most critical. The operative moved to the nightstand, where Senator Gray's reading glasses and a glass of water sat. He used a small, specialized forensic tool to collect minute fibers and biological residue—likely hair and skin cells—and then, with the precision of a surgeon, he moved to the body.

The video clearly showed the operative inserting the Gray's DNA under Sarah Jenkins' fingernails, precisely recreating the evidence of a "struggle." He finished by kicking the slippers neatly into place near the closet wall—the exact detail that had set off Anne's initial alarm.

The scene was, undeniably, staged. Senator Marcus David Gray was innocent of murder.

But the relief was short-lived.

"Wait, go back," Anne commanded, her voice barely a whisper. "Right there. When he finished staging the DNA."

Elias paused the video. The operative was now standing by the door.

"Look at the monitor rack behind him, just to the left of the door," Anne directed.

Elias zoomed in. The monitor rack, mostly out of sight, held a specialized, encrypted communications terminal. Written on a piece of adhesive tape stuck to the side of the terminal was a word: Perseus.

"Perseus," Elias repeated, typing the name rapidly into a global intelligence database. "It's the designation for a highly compartmented, foreign intelligence program. Russian-linked. They specialize in long-term asset development and political insertion. They don't just kill; they own the victim, the asset, and the entire political outcome."

The meaning was devastating. Senator Marcus David Gray hadn't killed his Chief of Staff. He *was* the asset. Sarah Jenkins, the victim, had likely been his controller or a member of the network who was liquidated when she became a liability or tried to defect. The murder trial itself was not the end goal, but the process—a mechanism to protect Gray, or more likely, to provide him with a perfect, public crisis that would insulate him from deeper investigation.

Anne stared at the screen, the truth cold and hard. The man she was chasing was part of a global conspiracy, and the man Charlotte Reed was defending was their political prize.

"They used the murder to clean up a political loose end and generate public sympathy for the asset," Anne concluded, rubbing her aching wrist. "And now, Judge Lomax is running interference to keep the focus narrow, away from the Serbian money and the rest of the network."

Elias closed the video file and removed the SD card, placing it in a titanium, tamper-proof container. "This evidence is a ticking bomb, Anne. It can't go to the D.C. police, and it sure as hell can't go to Georgia Wright. They're all compromised, or controlled."

"The only one fighting this fix is Charlotte Reed," Anne murmured. "She's fighting Judge Lomax with legal maneuvers, convinced Gray is being framed by a political enemy. She is the only independent force with the power to derail the trial from the inside."

"You're suggesting an alliance?" Elias looked appalled. "With the high-priced defense attorney who's getting the actual asset off the hook?"

"I'm suggesting we use her perfect record and her legal access to the system," Anne corrected him. "I can't use the video in court. The chain of custody is broken—I broke into Townhome 21, and the operative knows I have it. I'd be facing federal charges, and the video would be tossed instantly. But Charlotte can use information derived from the video to destroy Georgia Wright's *staged timeline.* She can attack the methodology and timing of the murder, driving the focus to the fact that someone else was in the room, without ever revealing the existence of 'Perseus' or the political treason."

Anne stood up, despite the shooting pain in her arm. "She fights the murder charge; we fight the treason charge. We feed her just enough information to keep Gray safe from conviction but simultaneously give her the tools to expose the judicial fix and the network's existence."

14:00—Defense Command Center, D.C.

Charlotte was exhausted but running on sheer willpower. She had spent the morning on the phone with her New York team, coordinating the deep dive into 21 Holdings LLC and the connections to Judge Lomax's political intermediaries. The Judge's denial of her motion yesterday had solidified her conviction: the Bench was actively protecting the Senator's hidden masters.

Rupert McCallister was pacing, nervous energy radiating off him. "Charlotte, you can't keep the press waiting on the arraignment decision. They're expecting a statement on the Judge's denial."

"Let them wait," Charlotte snapped, her eyes fixed on the limited financial documents Georgia Wright had been compelled to provide—Sarah Jenkins' personal checking and her campaign expense reports. "Look at this, Rupert. It's nothing. Sarah Jenkins was paying her rent, her dry cleaning, and making three campaign-related wire transfers to a D.C.-based media consulting firm for 'image management.'"

"So?"

"So, she was wiring $450,000 to a shell company in Belgrade three weeks ago, but she couldn't afford to pay for her $600 monthly parking space, which was paid for by the Senator's official campaign account," Charlotte pointed out, tapping the report. "This is a ghost account. The account that sent the money to Serbia is not the one she used to buy coffee. It's a separate ledger, which Gray's campaign handed over only because the Judge forced them to."

The financial record confirmed Gray was right: he was being framed, but the frame was designed to look like a spousal murder to hide a larger, financial conspiracy.

Her secure line—the one she never shared with any client—flashed with an unregistered number. It was a single, cryptic text message.

21: Alley. Midnight. Solo. Your last chance to save your client.

Charlotte's blood ran cold. *21.* Townhome 21. This was Detective Anne Austin. The Lead Investigator, the woman who had built the case against her client. The risk was monumental. If this was a trap, her career, her perfect record, and potentially her life were over. But the message contained the number 21, the same number Wilfred's memo had referenced, the same number her team was tying to the Serbian money. It was the nexus of the conspiracy.

She looked at Rupert. "I need you to handle the press conference. Emphasize the denial of Wright's discovery motion as evidence that the State has a weak, circumstantial case. Do not mention Wilfred. Do not mention Lomax. I have a critical, private meeting."

"A meeting? At midnight?" Rupert asked, raising a skeptical eyebrow.

"Something Wilfred would have handled," Charlotte said, grabbing her coat and briefcase. "Something that will either win this case, or end it."

00:00—The Alleyway Behind Townhome 21, Georgetown

The alley was dark, cold, and silent, the air heavy with the recent rain. Charlotte stood exactly where Anne Austin had nearly died hours before. She was alone. She had left her phone in the car, bringing only a small, powerful flashlight and her briefcase.

A figure emerged from the deeper shadows, moving stiffly. Detective Anne Austin. She was wearing a thick, oversized coat, but even in the poor light, Charlotte could see the bruising on her neck and the makeshift splint binding her wrist.

"Reed," Anne rasped, her voice harsh.

"Detective Austin. You risk everything to be here. I risk everything to trust you," Charlotte said, keeping her voice level, professional. "Make your case fast. Why aren't you arresting me for obstruction, and why should I believe the Lead Investigator of the State's case when she says she wants to help the defense?"

Anne stepped fully into the thin beam of light from a distant streetlight. Her eyes, shadowed with fatigue and pain, were steady.

"Because Senator Gray did not kill Sarah Jenkins, Ms. Reed," Anne stated. "I know it. I have the evidence. The crime scene was a professional fabrication designed to frame him and shut down the real investigation."

Charlotte's composure wavered for a millisecond. She had suspected it, but hearing the Lead Detective admit the case was a lie was staggering. "The DNA evidence?"

"Staged. Post-mortem. I have surveillance video that shows the real killer, an operative using a key to enter the room, incapacitate the victim, and then plant the Senator's DNA under her nails," Anne revealed, giving away the core mechanism of the crime but not the political context.

"A key," Charlotte whispered. "She let him in, or someone close did. And the motive? Why frame Gray?"

Anne looked Charlotte dead in the eye. "That's your blind spot, Reed. The motive isn't murder; it's political. The money you're chasing to Serbia, the shell company, the Judge. They're all connected. You are defending a man who is the face of a network, and the murder trial is the curtain they're hiding behind."

Charlotte pulled Wilfred's crumpled note from her pocket, the three words burned into her memory. "Don't trust the Bench. Judge Lomax denied both our key motions today, ensuring the case stays narrow and in his court. He's running interference."

"Exactly," Anne confirmed. "Lomax is the 21st Juror. He is

controlling the game. If you try to introduce my surveillance video, the entire thing is dismissed due to my illegal acquisition and broken chain of custody. You lose the trial, and the network walks free with Gray as their President."

Charlotte's mind raced, synthesizing the financial data, Wilfred's warning, and Anne's deadly truth. This was no longer about a perfect record. This was espionage, and she was trapped in the middle.

"What is the play, Detective?" Charlotte demanded.

"You attack the time of death and the method of death," Anne explained, her voice firm despite the pain. "You use the truth about the staged DNA and the pre-existing incapacitation—the strange compound Dr. Mirza found—to introduce reasonable doubt about the timeline. You make the prosecution prove that Senator Gray, despite his claimed movements, *could not* have left the room before the killer entered."

"And you?"

"I feed you the evidence you need, unofficially," Anne said. "I run the investigation you can't run. I'll follow the operative, and I'll find out who gave him the key. You use the courtroom as the spotlight. You keep the trial alive, but you attack the foundation of their case until they're forced to move the focus—and the Judge—off the bench."

It was a dangerous, extralegal alliance. A defense attorney and the lead homicide detective, conspiring to manipulate a murder trial to expose a political conspiracy.

Charlotte extended her hand, not for a handshake, but as a silent, professional acknowledgment. "You give me the next piece of evidence that destroys the prosecution's timeline. I'll give you the network's financial map. We don't speak again unless it's via my secure text, using the code phrase: *Perseus Protocol.*"

Anne nodded, her eyes fierce. She was fighting the pain, the fear, and the entire weight of the system, but she was back in the fight.

"Perseus Protocol," Anne confirmed. "The arraignment is next week. I'll have something for you before then. Something that will put the killer, and the Judge, on the defensive."

Anne turned and melted back into the deep shadows of the alley. Charlotte watched her go, then pulled her phone from her coat pocket. The adrenaline was back, cold and necessary. She had a new partner, a broken arm, and a secret video showing the murder, none of which she could legally use.

She walked quickly back to her car, already calculating the legal maneuvers needed to bring Dr. Amir Mirza back to the stand for the preliminary hearing, armed with the knowledge that the toxicology report was the key to unlocking the entire, staged crime. The stakes had been reset. It was a race between Charlotte Reed's mind and the shadow network's assassins.

CHAPTER 7

The Ghost in the Blood (Charlotte Reed & Dr. Amir Mirza)

08:30—Defense Command Center, D.C.

Charlotte Reed felt the cold burn of the adrenaline crash that follows a midnight alliance. She was running on three hours of sleep and the chilling knowledge that her new co-conspirator, Detective Anne Austin, was bruised, likely fractured, and running from a highly trained operative known only by the shadow designation Perseus. The stakes were no longer the Senator's freedom; they were the exposure of a deep state insertion.

Her task today was surgical: to use the information Anne had risked her life for—the fact that Sarah Jenkins was incapacitated before the struggle—and introduce it legally through the prosecution's own witness, Dr. Amir Mirza, without ever mentioning Townhome 21 or the illegal video.

She had spent the early morning hours reviewing Dr. Mirza's official preliminary autopsy report, focusing on the five pages dedicated to the blood toxicology screen. The report dismissed the presence of the minute, unidentified trace compound as 'potential environmental contamination.' Charlotte knew better. It was the key to the entire staged crime.

It was the 'ghost in the blood'—the chemical footprint of the professional killer.

Rupert McCallister watched her, sipping an organic green juice, his expression a mixture of fascination and professional unease.

"I still maintain this is a reckless strategy, Charlotte," Rupert said, adjusting his tie. "You've filed three motions in twenty-four hours, the third of which accused the Judge of impropriety. Now, you're dragging the medical examiner back to the preliminary hearing to grill him on a trace element the State has already discounted. You are handing Georgia Wright a slam-dunk objection on relevance."

Charlotte looked up, her expression lethal. "Relevance is whatever I make it, Rupert. Dr. Mirza testified the time of death coincided with the Senator's return to the room and that the DNA under the victim's nails was consistent with a struggle. The prosecution's entire case is built on passion, rage, and a struggle. I will obliterate that motive."

"But how? You have no expert witness of your own yet to challenge Mirza's conclusion that the trace element is contamination."

"I don't need my own expert. I need Dr. Mirza to testify to the *plausibility* of an alternate scenario," Charlotte explained, drawing a careful line on her legal pad. "The moment he admits that compound, whatever it is, *could* have induced temporary paralysis or extreme disorientation, the narrative shifts from murder-in-a-rage to premeditated execution and staging. That single admission is enough to create reasonable doubt and force the jury to consider a third party—a shadow figure."

Charlotte looked down at the file, remembering Wilfred Sinclair's hurried departure and the terrifying note. Wilfred had set her up perfectly to find the Belgrade money, but he had also left her to fight a Judge who was now confirmed as an opponent. She had to use this moment to force Lomax's hand.

"Get your files ready, Rupert. The goal is simple: to make Dr. Mirza look more like an advocate for the State's narrative than an impartial scientist. Lomax will hate it. Which is precisely the point."

Direct Examination: The Immutability of DNA (Georgia Wright)

10:00—District Courtroom 302, D.C.

The courtroom was heavy with anticipation. The media frenzy outside the courthouse had only intensified following Judge Lomax's conflicting rulings the day before, which everyone interpreted as a sign of high political turmoil within the case.

Georgia Wright, the ADA, approached the podium, her sharp, focused gaze passing over Charlotte Reed without acknowledgment. She had spent the last twenty-four hours trying to process the chilling realization that she, too, was being watched, managed, and controlled. The image of the imposing operative in the gallery doorway remained vividly in her mind. Her fury at Charlotte was now secondary to a growing, cold fear of her own exposure.

She needed a clean win, a moment of undeniable clarity to re-establish the State's dominance. Dr. Amir Mirza, the distinguished medical examiner, was her tool.

"Dr. Mirza," Georgia began, her voice professional and resonant, "for the benefit of the Court, please describe your primary forensic findings regarding the victim, Sarah Jenkins."

Dr. Mirza, dignified and detached in his role, summarized the findings succinctly. "The primary cause of death was asphyxia due to strangulation. The time of death, based on core body temperature and rigor mortis progression, occurred between 03:00 and 03:30 a.m. The force applied was significant and immediate."

Georgia moved quickly to the core of the State's narrative: the struggle.

"And during the struggle that led to the victim's death, did you recover any trace evidence that would indicate who the aggressor was?"

"Yes, Ms. Wright. Beneath the fingernails of the deceased, we recovered epithelial cells and hair fragments consistent with the DNA profile of Senator Marcus David Gray. This is conclusive evidence of a physical, violent struggle between the victim and the defendant in the moments leading up to her death."

"So, Dr. Mirza, based on the totality of the evidence—the violent nature of the death, the transfer of the defendant's DNA during a struggle, and the timing of the incident—is there any doubt in your professional opinion that Senator Gray was the perpetrator of this crime?"

Dr. Mirza shifted slightly, his gaze briefly flickering toward the ceiling. He was bound by the scientific evidence in the official report, but the scientist in him was battling the political pressure he knew was hovering over the case. He swallowed.

"Based *only* on the evidence presented in the official report and the high-probability timing of the incident, Ms. Wright," he replied, his voice measured, "the evidence is overwhelmingly consistent with a fatal confrontation involving Senator Gray."

Georgia Wright smiled, a tight, thin curve of victory. She had sealed the narrative. She stepped back.

"The State rests its examination on this point, Your Honor. The DNA does not lie."

Charlotte rose immediately, her movement smooth and predatory. She approached the stand, ignoring the tense, expectant silence of the courtroom.

The Cross-Examination: The Incapacitation

Charlotte didn't start with the blood; she started with the environment—a tactic learned from Anne Austin's initial observations.

"Good morning, Dr. Mirza," Charlotte said, her voice courteous, almost disarmingly so. "You are a scientist, bound only by objective data, correct?"

"Absolutely, Ms. Reed."

"And a key component of objective data is the *absence* of expected evidence, is it not? The things that *should* be there, but are not?"

Mirza paused, detecting the shift in approach. "That is correct."

"Please refer to your findings on the victim's defensive wounds. Were there any bruises, lacerations, or breaks consistent with a desperate, all-out struggle for life?"

"The victim had minor bruising on her upper arms, consistent with someone being restrained, but surprisingly few defensive wounds on her hands or forearms, yes."

"Surprising, given the fatal nature of the attack?"

"Relatively, yes. We would typically expect more extreme signs of resistance."

"Let's discuss the scene. Detective Austin's initial report, which you reviewed, noted that the victim's slippers were found neatly tucked against the wall, six feet from the body. Do you recall that detail?"

"I do."

"In a moment of violent, desperate confrontation—a struggle that resulted in fatal strangulation—would you expect the victim, upon falling, to have the situational awareness and muscular control to arrange her footwear neatly against the wall?"

Dr. Mirza hesitated, running a hand over his chin. "That is highly unlikely, Ms. Reed. The position of the slippers suggests they were placed there, or that the victim was not in a state of conscious, defensive struggle when the final incident occurred."

The courtroom stirred. Charlotte had just introduced the word *placed*—the suggestion of staging—without relying on the illegal video.

"Now, let's talk about the DNA under the fingernails—the central tenet of the State's case," Charlotte continued, maintaining her calm, measured pace. "You testified that this evidence is consistent with a struggle. But DNA transfer is a common, everyday occurrence, is it not?"

"It is."

"Could the Senator's DNA have been transferred during the heated argument he claims he had with the victim moments earlier—when she grabbed his arm and he pulled away?"

"It is biologically possible, yes. The epithelial cells could have transferred then."

"And if the DNA was transferred earlier, and the victim was later incapacitated, and *then* the struggle was manufactured, the DNA would still be present beneath the nails, correct?"

"The DNA would be present, yes."

Charlotte pressed harder, leaning on the podium, forcing Dr. Mirza to confront the anomaly he had discounted.

"Doctor, turn now to the blood toxicology report, specifically the section detailing the 'Unidentified Trace Compound.' You listed it as 'potential environmental contamination.' Can you describe the quantity of this contamination?"

"It was present in only a very minute, trace amount, Ms. Reed. Statistically, it's often disregarded."

"Yet you still noted it," Charlotte observed. "In a case involving the death of a Chief of Staff to a Presidential candidate, in a secured residence, you chose not to ignore it. Why?"

Dr. Mirza looked visibly uncomfortable. "Because its molecular structure was not immediately identifiable, which is unusual for common environmental contaminants like cleaning agents or dust."

Charlotte seized the opening. "So, it was unusual. Now, let's delve into the nature of the unusual. Dr. Mirza, based on your years of experience, if that trace compound, despite its minute quantity, was *not* contamination, but was instead a high-potency, fast-acting neurotoxin or muscle paralytic, what effect would it have had on Ms. Jenkins' ability to defend herself?"

Georgia Wright finally exploded. "Objection, Your Honor! Speculation! This line of questioning requires the witness to abandon all scientific protocol and enter the realm of fantasy!"

Judge Lomax, who had been watching Charlotte with icy intent, raised his hand sharply. "Ms. Reed, you are testing the boundaries of relevance. Confine your questions to the contents of the report."

"I am confined to the report, Your Honor," Charlotte countered smoothly, turning back to the Judge. "The trace element *is* in the report. I am simply asking the witness to provide a professional hypothesis on its *potential* function. Dr. Mirza, can you state under oath that the presence of that unknown compound *absolutely* could not have been a high-potency agent designed to induce temporary paralysis?"

Dr. Mirza was caught in the ethical vice. He couldn't lie, and he couldn't rule out the possibility Charlotte had introduced. He looked at Judge Lomax, then back at Charlotte.

"I... I cannot rule out that possibility entirely," Dr. Mirza admitted, his voice barely audible in the packed courtroom. "The molecular structure was unknown. A high-potency agent requires only trace amounts to be effective."

"Thank you, Doctor," Charlotte said softly, the victory already won. "You have now conceded that the State's key witness cannot rule out the possibility that the victim was pre-incapacitated by an unknown agent before the fatal strangulation, which would suggest the DNA evidence of a struggle was *staged*, and that a third party was involved."

Georgia Wright was shouting for a mistrial declaration. The courtroom was chaos.

Judge Lomax brought the gavel down with a series of sharp, violent cracks. "Order! Order! That is enough, Ms. Reed! The Court notes for the record that the defense's line of questioning regarding the trace element is based on reckless speculation and is not to be used by the jury to infer the existence of an unknown third party. It is to be considered only as part of a general, theoretical challenge to the time of death! I am striking the witness's last two responses from the record!"

The Judge was furious, his face white with rage and fear. Charlotte had done it. She had forced the Judge to intervene in the evidence, confirming for her—and for Anne, who would be reading the transcripts—that he was indeed protecting the core mechanism of the crime.

"Your Honor, with all due respect, I submit that the witness's testimony regarding the plausible incapacitation of the victim destroys the State's theory of motive and opportunity and is grounds for immediate summary judgment of acquittal," Charlotte stated firmly, despite the Judge's threats.

Lomax slammed the gavel again. "Motion denied! Get out of my courtroom, Ms. Reed! The Court is in recess until the arraignment!"

Charlotte gathered her papers, her hands trembling slightly, not from fear, but from the exhilaration of the victory. The perfect record was safe, and the first major twist had been executed. The *Perseus* network knew they had a problem.

Tracking the Phantom (Detective Anne Austin & Elias Vance)

11:15—An Isolated Data Center, Maryland

Miles away from the courtroom drama, Anne Austin watched the live transcript of the cross-examination on a secured laptop, wincing at every crack of Judge Lomax's gavel. She had a bag of ice strapped to her fractured wrist, and a grim smile touched her lips.

"She did it, Elias. She made him say it. 'Pre-incapacitated.' The prosecution's narrative is dead," Anne said, pointing at the transcript.

Elias Vance, running complex algorithms on a bank of servers, didn't look up. "The Judge's intervention confirms our theory: Lomax is running clean-up for the network. But Lomax is just the controller. We need the trigger man—the operative who attacked you."

Elias had been running the data from the SD card. He found a critical, microscopic piece of metadata: a temporary, non-encrypted login key the operative had used for twenty seconds on the Perseus terminal to run a quick system check before leaving Townhome 21.

"I traced the momentary login key," Elias announced, his voice low and intense. "It's a standard, disposable access point, but they made a mistake. When the operative signed in, his system pinged a single, known D.C. IP address for verification. It's not the Belgrade HQ, Anne. It's local."

He pulled up a digital map of Washington D.C. A single, blinking red dot appeared in a secluded, wealthy neighborhood in Northwest D.C.

"This is the home address of the login key's registered owner," Elias stated. "A man named Joseph Lomax Jr."

Anne stared at the screen, a cold realization settling in her stomach. "Joseph Lomax Jr. The Judge's son. That can't be a coincidence. The Judge isn't just controlling the trial; he's covering for his own flesh and blood."

"The login key confirms it," Elias said, zooming in on the property profile. "Joseph Lomax Jr. has a known criminal history—minor fraud charges from five years ago that vanished from the public record. Now he lives in a high-security residence funded by an untraceable trust."

Anne's mind reeled, connecting the political plot to the personal betrayal. The Perseus Protocol hadn't just recruited a Senator; they had recruited a desperate, indebted son and blackmailed the father—Judge Joseph Lomax—into ensuring the murder trial went exactly as planned. The Judge wasn't evil; he was compromised, leveraged by the life of his child.

"The son killed Sarah Jenkins and staged the scene," Anne murmured, piecing together the events. "And the father, to protect the son from the consequences of murder, is presiding over the trial. He is the ultimate, conflicted 21st Juror."

"The Justice Department won't touch a sitting Federal Judge, Anne. Not without irrefutable proof of bribery or coercion. We have the video, but it's inadmissible, and the son is the killer, not the Judge."

"No," Anne corrected him, grabbing her coat. "The son is the killer, but the father is the *traitor*. Lomax is using his judicial position to protect a foreign asset and a state-sponsored murder. That's treason."

She looked at Elias, her eyes burning with determination. "We have to find the son, Joseph Lomax Jr. He is the key to unlocking the Judge, who is the key to unlocking the entire Perseus network. Give me the tactical data on that residence. I'm going in."

"Anne, you are fractured, exhausted, and now you're going after the son of a federal judge, who is a professional assassin linked to Russian intelligence? This is suicide."

"It's the only way to save Charlotte Reed's life, and stop a puppet President," Anne insisted, pulling on her gloves with difficulty. She activated her secure phone and typed a message, the only way she had to communicate with her new, secret partner.

To: Charlotte Reed. Code: Perseus Protocol. Message: The key is family. Lomax Jr. is the trigger. Find his connection to Gray's campaign manager, Sarah Jenkins.

Anne Austin left the data center, heading toward Northwest D.C. She knew the mission was insane, but Charlotte Reed had just dismantled the prosecution's timeline. It was Anne's turn to dismantle the network's structure.

CHAPTER 8

The Vanishing Trail (Charlotte Reed)

18:00—Defense Command Center, D.C.

Charlotte returned to the conference room, buoyed by the devastating cross-examination victory, only to find the new text message waiting for her: *Perseus Protocol: The key is family. Lomax Jr. is the trigger. Find his connection to Gray's campaign manager, Sarah Jenkins.*

The name hit her like a punch: Lomax Jr. The Judge's son. A powerful, immediate connection to the judicial fix.

She immediately pulled up her team's financial report on 21 Holdings LLC and the single, archival photo of Judge Lomax shaking hands with the Russian oligarch's intermediary. She looked at Rupert McCallister, who was now utterly devoted to her aggressive strategy.

"Rupert, I need you to run a deep, immediate background check on Joseph Lomax Jr. Any current addresses, past arrests, financial records, and—most importantly—any possible social connection to Sarah Jenkins."

"Lomax Jr.? Why? He's irrelevant, Charlotte. The Judge just confirmed he's protecting the State by restricting your cross-examination. Why the son?"

"Because the Bench is comprised of two people, Rupert. The man in the black robe, and the man he's terrified of losing," Charlotte explained, rubbing her temples. "I'll tell you more when I have the data."

While Rupert initiated the Lomax Jr. search, Charlotte turned her attention back to the missing partner and the financial conspiracy.

"Ben, what have you found on the $450,000 wire transfer from Sarah Jenkins to 21 Holdings in Belgrade?" Charlotte asked her paralegal team leader via video conference.

Ben, who looked like he hadn't slept in three days, shook his head. "The trail is cold, Charlotte. We've managed to break through layers of shell corporations—Panama, Cyprus, Malta—but the money vanished when it hit the Belgrade receiving bank. It was immediately converted to cryptocurrency and routed through an untraceable peer-to-peer exchange network."

"So, it disappeared?"

"No, not disappeared," Ben corrected, his voice strained. "It was *liquidated* by the single person who had the final access key to the 21 Holdings master account. The funds were then immediately wired to a small, private D.C. address. It was a one-time, highly unusual transaction."

Charlotte felt a sudden, terrifying premonition. "Which D.C. address?"

Ben pulled up the final transaction detail. "A discreet, anonymous luxury condominium complex in Georgetown. Apartment 1205. The address is listed as the legal residence of Wilfred Sinclair."

Charlotte's blood ran cold. The man who had given her the

initial financial tip, who had forced her to see the Serbian link and accept the case, was the same man who had liquidated the entire fund and disappeared. He hadn't fled the network; he had *robbed* it. The entire Serbian money trail, the entire financial motive, led directly back to her trusted partner.

"Wilfred didn't run from the network, Ben," Charlotte whispered, the true, horrifying motive clicking into place. "He ran *with* the network's money. He was Sarah Jenkins' contact, running the money for Perseus. But when they killed Sarah, he knew he was next. So he took the funds, gave me the tip, and framed the Senator's defense as his last act of chaos, hoping to buy himself time to vanish."

"But the note, Charlotte," Rupert interjected, looking up from his laptop, having overheard the conversation. "The note: *Don't trust the Bench.* Why would he warn you about Lomax if he was the thief?"

Charlotte stared at the Belgrade transaction details on the screen. "Because he *knew* Lomax was compromised, and he knew I was the only person ruthless enough to leverage the Judge into giving him the time he needed. Wilfred didn't care if Gray was convicted. He just needed the trial to become so focused on the political frame-up that the network wouldn't have the bandwidth to hunt him and the money down immediately."

Her phone buzzed. It was Rupert's background check on the Judge's son.

"Charlotte, I have the report on Joseph Lomax Jr.," Rupert said, his voice laced with disbelief. "He lives in a secured home in Northwest D.C., and his past criminal record for fraud was completely expunged five years ago. But I found one other thing. His only listed employment in the last decade? He was a security consultant for Senator Marcus David Gray's presidential campaign, working under Sarah Jenkins, precisely at the time the Belgrade transfers were taking place."

The last piece of the immediate puzzle snapped into place, cementing the terrifying confluence of the legal, financial, and personal treason:

1. The Killer: Joseph Lomax Jr. (the Judge's son, the operative, the security consultant).
2. The Target/Victim: Sarah Jenkins (the Chief of Staff, the money handler).
3. The Traitor/Thief: Wilfred Sinclair (Charlotte's partner, the master account holder).
4. The Compromised Judge: Joseph Lomax Sr. (leveraged by his son's crime).
5. The Asset: Senator Marcus David Gray (the unknowing figurehead).

Charlotte's world had become a closed system of interlocking deceptions. The man she was defending was innocent of murder but guilty of being a puppet. The prosecutor was controlled. The Judge was blackmailed. And her partner was a thief on the run with foreign intelligence money.

She closed her briefcase, feeling the weight of the eight million dollars Gray had paid her. She was now the only honest, uncompromised piece of a massive, treasonous machine, but she was trapped.

"Rupert, cancel all future press briefings," Charlotte commanded. "You are officially running the standard defense. I need to know every single political pressure point, every financial weakness, and every vulnerability of Judge Joseph Lomax, Sr."

She pulled out her secure phone and typed a two-word message to Anne Austin, confirming the grim truth of her new enemy.

Charlotte Reed knew what she had to do next. She had to break the Judge, and she had to do it before the trial began. And the only way to break the Judge was through his weakness: his assassin son, Joseph Lomax Jr., the man Anne Austin was currently hunting. The endgame was beginning, and Charlotte had to move outside the law to save the rule of law itself.

CHAPTER 9

The Son and the Sin (Detective Anne Austin)

02:30—Northwest D.C. Residential Compound

The silence in the wealthy, tree-lined neighborhood was absolute, broken only by the distant, rhythmic cycling of a sprinkler system. Detective Anne Austin, dressed in black tactical gear borrowed from Elias Vance's supply closet, moved with the rigid, calculated caution of someone whose body was failing her, but whose mind was operating at peak efficiency.

The residence of Joseph Lomax Jr. was not a home; it was a fortress. Hidden behind a ten-foot stucco wall topped with razor wire and obscured by thick, manicured evergreens, the compound was a perfect representation of the man's shadowed existence—untraceable luxury guarded by paramilitary defenses.

Anne was running solely on the data Elias had provided: the exact location of the main power grid bypass, the frequency of the neighborhood patrol loops (which Lomax Jr. himself had likely programmed during his campaign security consultancy), and the fact that the compound relied on a sophisticated, laser-grid perimeter alarm, not pressure plates.

Her fractured wrist pulsed with a sickening, metronomic agony, constrained in a carbon-fiber brace Elias had secured. She had taken a cocktail of painkillers that dulled the immediate sharpness but left a thick, oily film of nausea coating her thoughts. She knew she was operating at maybe sixty percent capacity. Her only advantage was surprise, and the knowledge of her opponent's methodology.

The killer is the son. The operative is the son. The revelation had given her focus, transforming the fight from a police investigation into a duel of personal necessity. If Lomax Jr. walked free, the network won. If she failed, Charlotte Reed would be next.

Anne reached the perimeter wall, the cold cement rough against her cheek. She could see the faint, almost invisible red shimmer of the laser grid four feet above the ground. She pulled a can of industrial aerosol paint from her pack, aiming low. She sprayed a quick, horizontal line just above the grid, creating a thin, white mist. The mist immediately dissipated the red light, allowing her to see the pattern of the beams. The beams were set too low, designed to detect intruders running along the ground, not a vertical ascent. A rookie mistake, or perhaps a sign of Lomax Jr.'s confidence in his own wall.

She threw a grappling hook—a featherlight, high-tension carbon-fiber tool—over the wall. It caught silently on the inner ridge. Anne tested the weight, wincing as the strain pulled at her compromised forearm.

She climbed, focusing on placing her weight entirely on her left side, ascending the rough stucco like a spider. Every shift of weight sent a searing jolt through her right wrist, causing her to grit her teeth against the pain. She moved with meticulous slowness, her mind ticking off the seconds. She had a ten-minute window between patrol sweeps.

She dropped silently onto the soft, manicured grass inside the compound. The house itself was a sprawling, dark structure, all black glass and geometric angles—a brutalist design meant to intimidate.

Elias had warned her about the final layer: the internal magnetic locks. "They run on a secondary, dedicated power line. You can cut the main house power, but the doors stay locked. You need the biometric signature or the security master key."

Anne didn't have the key. She moved to the side of the house, where the secondary maintenance access door was located. It was steel, thick and windowless. She pulled out a small, portable power inverter and a fiber optic scope. She threaded the scope through the minute gap between the door and the frame, illuminating the internal mechanism. The magnetic plates were secured by four heavy bolts and a complex wiring harness.

She spent five agonizing minutes mapping the internal wiring schematic on her tablet, comparing it to the blueprints Elias had illegally sourced from the building's contractor. She found the fail-safe wire—the one designed to disconnect the primary magnetic lock without tripping the silent alarm.

She clipped the wire with surgical precision. The only sound was a soft, high-pitched *thunk* as the magnetic field collapsed. The door was now secured only by a simple deadbolt.

Anne picked the deadbolt in thirty seconds, a task made immensely difficult by the loss of fine motor control in her right hand. She used her mouth and her left index finger to manipulate the tension wrench and the pick. When the lock finally gave, she pushed the door inward, slipping into the dark, silent kitchen.

This interior was even colder and more clinical than

Townhome 21. It was an environment built for efficiency and absence.

Anne drew her backup weapon—a lightweight Glock 19 she had strapped to her thigh—holding it steady in her left hand. She moved through the house, clearing rooms with the practiced discipline of a veteran detective, relying on sound and shadow.

The main floor was dedicated to austere luxury: an empty living room, a dining room set for six but clearly never used, and a glass-walled office overlooking a sunken patio.

Anne entered the office. This was where the man lived, where the operative planned. The desk was bare, but the computer setup was anything but. Four monitors, all black, were linked to a tower sitting inside a custom-built, soundproofed server box.

She moved to the computer, quickly bypassing the screen lock with a portable decryption key from Elias. The home screen was a standard Windows desktop, but the folders were the real story. Three prominent icons dominated the screen: Gray Campaign Files (Archived), 21 Ledger Backup, and Sinclair Target.

Anne's breath hitched. *Sinclair Target.* Lomax Jr. wasn't just working for Perseus; he was actively tracking Wilfred, who had just stolen the network's money. This confirmed the double-cross.

She opened the Sinclair Target folder. It was dense with surveillance data: GPS coordinates, burner phone logs, and highly detailed digital photographs of Wilfred Sinclair at various undisclosed locations—a marina in Miami, a quiet cafe in Zurich, and finally, a luxury villa on the coast of Malta. Lomax Jr. was closing in on the thief.

Anne scrolled down, searching for any direct evidence of Judge Lomax Sr.'s coercion. She found it buried in a subfolder labeled Family Documents.

The folder contained only two files. The first was a Wire Transfer Receipt for $500,000 sent from a D.C. trust account registered under *J.L. Senior* to a Belgrade-linked offshore bank account—dated five years ago. This was the money used to pay off Lomax Jr.'s fraud victims and wipe his criminal record clean, confirming the initial leverage used by Perseus. The Judge had been compromised for years, paying hush money to protect his son.

The second file was a recent, internal campaign memo: a short, encrypted file sent from Lomax Jr.'s private security terminal to Sarah Jenkins' personal phone two days before the murder. Anne ran a quick, on-the-spot decryption.

The memo read: *Subject: Operational Readiness. The Asset's policy reversal is not acceptable. Jenkins is panicking about exposure. Her payment to 21 Holdings is confirmed. The retrieval sequence—PERSEUS PROTOCOL, Phase One—is green-lit for 03:00. Ensure scene staging is flawless. Target: Jenkins. Objective: Re-stabilize Asset Gray and leverage the Bench.*

It was the smoking gun. It detailed the entire plot: Sarah Jenkins, the victim, was paying off the network, but her last-minute panic over Gray's policy reversal had triggered her own execution. Lomax Jr. was the executioner, and the goal was to leverage his father, the Judge, to control the resulting trial.

Anne knew she couldn't copy the files. The computer was certainly rigged with a remote monitoring system that would alert Lomax Jr. the instant she tried to transfer large data packets. She needed to immobilize the computer, secure a single, portable piece of evidence, and get out.

She grabbed a small, customized USB drive from her pack—a military-grade hardware key that Elias had configured. It wasn't designed to steal data; it was designed to *corrupt* data on contact. She jammed it into the server tower's main processing port. A thin, whining sound emanated from the tower as the drive began its work, destabilizing the encrypted hard drives.

Just as the whine peaked, Anne heard the soft, distant *click* of the magnetic lock on the exterior door. Lomax Jr. was back.

Anne pulled the USB drive out and flattened herself against the cold, interior wall of the office, Glock raised, her left arm trembling with the strain. She could hear the smooth, quiet sounds of the operative moving through the house. He was thorough, professional, and terrifyingly fast.

He entered the dining room, moving toward the office. Anne could see the shadow of his tactical boot under the door.

Confrontation: The Trigger Man

The door opened slowly. Joseph Lomax Jr. was wearing a thick, black waterproof coat and gloves, the same tactical gear as the night before. His face was unmasked now, revealing a set of sharp, intelligent features that were chillingly familiar: the same high forehead and piercing, dark eyes as his father, Judge Joseph Lomax. He looked like a handsome, ruthless version of the man on the bench.

Lomax Jr. did not immediately enter. He paused, his head cocked slightly, having instantly sensed the disturbance in the air. He saw the subtle, almost invisible sheen of oil on the deadbolt from Anne's lock-picking tool.

He knew she was there.

"Detective Austin," Lomax Jr. said, his voice a low, cultured baritone, completely different from the strained whisper he had used the night before. "I should have known you'd return to the scene of your failure. You broke your arm, stole an SD card, and now you've broken into my home. A tragic end to a promising career."

He stepped into the office, his eyes immediately assessing the room. He saw the open server box and the subtle glow of the corrupting USB drive's indicator light still reflecting on the casing. His eyes narrowed instantly, and the mask of composure shattered.

"You *fool*," he hissed, lunging for the server tower. "You've corrupted the 21 Ledger! Do you know what you've done?"

This was Anne's chance. She didn't shoot. Shooting would alert the entire D.C. police force, and the Judge would have her arrested before she could breathe the word *Perseus*. She needed leverage, not a body count.

As Lomax Jr. reached for the server, desperately trying to salvage the corrupted hard drives, Anne moved. She didn't rely on strength; she relied on her tactical knowledge of his pain points. She knew from the fight in the alley that his right knee was momentarily injured when the table hit it.

She dropped to her good knee and fired a single shot, not at Lomax Jr., but at the high-end air conditioning unit built into the wall directly behind him. The shot was loud, deafening in the enclosed space, and the projectile shattered the unit, sending a massive spray of cold, pressurized refrigerant gas and shrapnel into the office.

Lomax Jr. cried out, turning away from the blast, shielding his face from the shards of metal and the blinding white gas.

Anne used the second of confusion to seize the most valuable item on the desk—a small, highly encrypted, black laptop labeled simply *J.L. Senior*. It was the only item not tied directly to the main server rack, likely a redundant backup for the Judge.

She moved with the speed of desperation, grabbing the laptop in her left hand, and scrambling out of the office, heading back toward the maintenance door.

Lomax Jr. recovered quickly, wiping the stinging gas from his eyes. He saw the missing laptop. "The personal terminal! Stop her!"

He lunged after Anne, but she had reached the kitchen and jammed a chair under the dead-bolted door. It wouldn't hold him long, but it bought her precious seconds.

She scrambled out the maintenance door, resetting the deadbolt with a quick twist, and sprinted across the compound lawn, ignoring the white-hot pain shooting up her arm. She reached the wall, clipped the hook, and threw herself over, landing hard on the other side.

Lomax Jr. kicked the maintenance door open, emerging onto the lawn moments later. He saw the faint, swaying line of the grappling rope hanging over the wall. He knew he couldn't follow her now; the wall was too complex, and the sound of his forced entry might have alerted the next patrol. He cursed, turning back to the house. His entire digital ledger was corrupted, and the only backup—the personal terminal for the Judge—was gone.

Anne ran until she reached the safety of her parked, unmarked car six blocks away. She slammed the door shut, locking it, and slumped back into the seat, breathing hard. Her whole body shook violently, her arm throbbing with unbearable intensity. But cradled against her chest was the small, black laptop.

She had failed to capture the killer, but she had secured the leverage to break the network's control over the Judge.

She pulled out her phone, immediately dialing Elias Vance.

"Elias. It's done. Lomax Jr. is tracking Wilfred. And he confirmed the Perseus operation. I have the Judge's backup terminal. The network's control is on that drive."

"Get out of D.C., Anne. Now. They will be sweeping the grid for that laptop's GPS signal within the hour."

"I can't," Anne said, already driving toward the federal annex. "I need to leverage the Judge before the arraignment. I need Charlotte Reed."

03:15—Defense Command Center, D.C.

Charlotte Reed sat alone in the sterile conference room, the single overhead light casting stark shadows on the legal documents spread across the table. Rupert McCallister was asleep in a hotel room, and the Senator was sequestered. She was reviewing the Judge's financial history again, searching for any pressure point besides the blurry oligarch photo.

Her secure text flashed with the *Perseus Protocol* code. It was Anne Austin.

To: Charlotte Reed. Code: Perseus Protocol. Message: I have the personal terminal. Lomax Jr. is the operative. I have the evidence of the coercion. Get the Judge into a private meeting NOW. Tell him his son is running Phase One retrieval.

Charlotte read the message once, twice. *Personal terminal. Coercion. Phase One retrieval.* Anne had achieved the impossible: physical evidence linking the Judge's son to the murder and the network.

Charlotte immediately initiated a search on Phase One Retrieval. The term was military, not campaign. A quick cross-reference with known intelligence procedures confirmed it: Phase One Retrieval was the immediate, violent attempt to silence the key compromised individual—in this case, Wilfred Sinclair—and secure the stolen assets.

Wilfred was the primary target, and Lomax Jr. was the hunter.

Charlotte needed to break the Judge before his son executed her partner, or worse, before Lomax Jr. realized the gravity of the stolen laptop and came after the Judge's leverage.

She picked up the encrypted satellite phone. She had only one move left, a move that would violate every principle of ethical conduct, but one that was necessary to save the Senator and expose the network.

She dialed a deeply protected number—the private, off-the-record line for Judge Joseph Lomax, Sr.

The phone rang twice before a tired, deep voice answered. "Lomax."

"Judge Lomax, this is Charlotte Reed," she said, her voice sharp and devoid of warmth. "I apologize for the hour. But this is not a defense attorney calling her client's judge. This is a notification of impending constitutional crisis."

Lomax's tone immediately hardened. "Ms. Reed, you are in blatant violation of multiple rules of professional conduct by calling me outside of scheduled judicial hours. Whatever you have to say, save it for the arraignment."

"The arraignment will be too late, Your Honor," Charlotte countered, ignoring the threat. "Your son, Joseph Lomax Jr., has been identified as the operative responsible for the murder of Sarah Jenkins. He is currently running Phase One Retrieval to secure evidence stolen by my partner, Wilfred Sinclair. I know you paid $500,000 to cover his past fraud five years ago, and I know that payment was the leverage used by the Perseus network to force you to control this trial.”

She heard the sharp intake of breath on the other end. The Judge didn't hang up. He was listening, paralyzed by the sudden, terrifying exposure.

“I have the personal terminal, Judge,” Charlotte continued, delivering the fatal blow. “The computer that contains all the evidence of your coercion and your son’s involvement. Detective Anne Austin secured it moments ago. I have proof of your son’s treason, and I will submit it to the Department of Justice within the hour, along with a motion for your immediate recusal and criminal investigation, unless we meet privately, *now*, before the arraignment.”

Lomax’s voice was a barely controlled whisper, stripped of all judicial authority. “You have ruined us, Ms. Reed. You have destroyed my life.”

“I’m trying to save your life, Judge,” Charlotte corrected him, the lie slipping out smoothly. “I want the Senator cleared of murder, and I want the Perseus network exposed, beginning with your son. I will trade you the terminal and the evidence of your coercion, and guarantee a path to save your son from the murder charge—but not the treason charge—if you guarantee me one thing: the instant recusal from this case and the naming of the operative who gave your son the key to Senator Gray’s townhome.”

The line remained silent for ten seconds—the longest silence in Charlotte’s life.

Finally, Judge Joseph Lomax, the conflicted 21st Juror, spoke, his voice cracked with absolute defeat. “Where do we meet, Ms. Reed? And where is my son?”

Charlotte looked at the stolen laptop on her desk, the cold, powerful light of its indicator reflecting in her eyes.

"We meet in my office, Judge. You come alone. And as for your son, he is currently hunting down my rogue partner. But he will be here soon. He has to be. Because he knows the key to his own freedom is now sitting on my desk."

Charlotte hung up, the final, reckless gamble executed. She now possessed the legal leverage, the political motive, and the physical evidence to break the Judge. The arraignment was hours away, and the courtroom was about to witness a collision of the legal and intelligence worlds that would determine the fate of the presidency.

CHAPTER 10

The Price of Treason (Charlotte Reed & Judge Lomax, Sr.)

04:30—Defense Command Center, D.C.

Charlotte Reed moved through the empty office suite with the unnerving stillness of a precision-engineered machine. The sun would not rise for hours, but the gravity of the impending meeting cast its own stark, fluorescent light over the conference room.

She was playing the most dangerous legal game of her life, holding the ultimate leverage against the man who represented the judicial branch: Judge Joseph Lomax, Sr. She had forced him into this illegal, pre-dawn meeting—a negotiation that was equal parts blackmail, intelligence operation, and existential defense of the American political system.

Charlotte had sent Rupert McCallister home hours ago with explicit, simple instructions: "Do not answer your phone, and do not come to the office until 8:00 a.m. If anyone asks, I'm working with the Senator on his statement." She had to isolate the operation, protect Rupert from knowledge that could implicate him, and secure the perimeter.

She was utterly alone.

In the center of the mahogany table sat the ransom: the small, black, encrypted laptop labeled *J.L. Senior.* Anne Austin had risked her life—and severely fractured her arm—to retrieve it, driving it directly to a pre-arranged, secure drop-off point near the annex an hour earlier. Charlotte hadn't seen Anne, only the laptop, resting inside a disposable gym bag.

Charlotte ran her hand across the cold, metallic casing of the Judge's terminal. It was a silent testament to the devastating truth: the man who wore the black robe was merely a slave to his own parental fear, leveraged by the treasonous actions of his son, Joseph Lomax Jr.

She had only two goals for the negotiation: Recusal and The Key.

Lomax's recusal had to be absolute, immediate, and based on "an undisclosed personal matter" to avoid exposing the network publicly before the proper authorities could be brought in. And The Key—the identity of the person who gave Lomax Jr. access to Senator Gray's private residence—was the essential next piece of evidence. It would confirm the depth of the penetration into Gray's circle.

Charlotte sat back, allowing the quiet hum of the building's air conditioning to fill the void. She thought of Wilfred Sinclair, the master manipulator, now a thief on the run, who had used his final moments of freedom to guide her to the truth. She thought of Detective Anne Austin, the righteous cop with a broken arm, now hiding in the shadows, waiting for the result of this duel. She was the fulcrum on which all their desperate gambits balanced.

A soft, electronic chime echoed from the main entrance of the suite—the signal Charlotte had pre-arranged with the Judge.

Charlotte rose, smoothing the imaginary wrinkles from her

jacket. She did not look like an attorney contemplating criminal blackmail; she looked like the calm embodiment of judicial consequence.

She opened the door herself.

Judge Joseph Lomax, Sr, stood on the threshold. He was dressed in a dark civilian coat, but even without his judicial robes, he carried the immense weight of his position. Yet, that weight was now crushing him. His face was gray, etched with exhaustion and profound anxiety. His eyes, usually sharp and penetrating, were clouded with despair. He looked frail, lost, and defeated.

Charlotte didn't offer a greeting, a handshake, or an apology. She simply opened the door wider and gestured toward the conference table.

"Your Honor. Thank you for coming. You came alone, as requested."

"I had no choice, Ms. Reed," Lomax's voice was hollow, stripped of its resonant authority, barely rising above a whisper. He stepped into the room, his eyes instantly fixing on the small, black laptop resting prominently on the table. He flinched, as if he had seen a venomous snake.

"Where is my son?" Lomax demanded, the father momentarily overriding the jurist.

"He is currently focused on an external, non-judicial matter—Phase One Retrieval—which is what the Perseus network calls the assassination and asset seizure of Wilfred Sinclair," Charlotte stated flatly, sitting down. She wanted to establish the brutal reality of the situation immediately. "Your son is a killer and an agent of a foreign power. He has your personal terminal on my table, and he is hunting my partner. The only reason he hasn't already returned here is because he is preoccupied, and because he doesn't yet know you came here."

Lomax stumbled into the chair opposite her, his dignity collapsing entirely. He buried his face in his hands, muffling a deep, ragged sound that was less a cry and more a sound of a magnificent, crumbling structure.

"My God," he whispered. "I tried to protect him. I just wanted to buy him time to run."

"You didn't buy him time, Your Honor. You sold the integrity of the American judicial system," Charlotte said, her voice devoid of emotion. "The $500,000 you transferred to Belgrade five years ago was the cost of clearing his fraud charges. That cleared the record, but it installed the leverage. They owned him; therefore, they owned you. The murder of Sarah Jenkins and the framing of Senator Gray was simply the price of his continued freedom."

Charlotte slid the *J.L. Senior* laptop closer to him, keeping her hands off it. "On this terminal, Judge, we have the Perseus memo detailing the entire operation: *Objective: Re-stabilize Asset Gray and leverage the Bench.* We have evidence of the financial coercion, and we have records that show your son, Joseph Lomax Jr., was the operative who staged the scene. We know you denied our motions not based on law, but to shield your son's involvement and prevent the case from leaving your control."

Lomax lifted his head, his eyes wet but blazing with a furious, desperate energy. "I am a Federal Judge, Ms. Reed! The sanctity of the Bench—you are blackmailing a servant of the law!"

"I am performing triage on a massive hemorrhage in the justice system, Your Honor," Charlotte countered, matching his intensity without raising her voice. "Your actions are treasonous. If I turn this laptop over to the Department of Justice, you face impeachment, disbarment, and a life sentence for obstruction and high treason. Your son faces the death penalty for state-sponsored murder. You and I are going to make a deal right now, a deal that ensures the network falls, and that your life, at least, is spared the worst of the fallout."

She leaned forward, dictating the terms like a lawyer delivering a closing argument.

"Term one: You will recuse yourself from the case of *State v. Gray* immediately, citing unavoidable, undisclosed personal necessity. This recusal must be filed by 8:00 a.m. today, before the arraignment. If you cite conflict of interest, the network will know the reason, and they will retaliate against your family, or against me."

Lomax nodded slowly, accepting the first condition with a painful grimace. "I will recuse. That is a given."

"Term two: I will give you this terminal," Charlotte continued, tapping the laptop. "And I will give you the proof of your son's location, so you can contact him and order him to stand down from the Phase One Retrieval operation. However, I will not destroy the evidence contained within. I will submit a complete mirror image of the drive to a trusted, high-ranking official within the FBI's counter-intelligence division, a person who will investigate the treason, not the murder. That person will be instructed to offer your son a deal: full immunity from the murder charge—since the evidence of coercion is strong—in exchange for full cooperation in exposing the entire Perseus network, including their Belgrade handlers and any other assets they have inside the D.C. government."

"Immunity for murder?" Lomax gasped, shocked.

"He is a coerced asset, Judge. The network made him do it. We need the network more than we need to send him to the chair for one murder," Charlotte said ruthlessly. "The goal is the network, not the son. He walks on the murder, but he must expose the treason. He gets his life, but he serves his country."

Lomax covered his face again, the moral calculus overwhelming him. His son was a professional killer, but he was also a hostage to a foreign power. Saving his life meant exposing the network.

"And what do you want for the Senator?" Lomax finally asked, his voice rough.

"The Senator is innocent of the murder charge, and I will clear him in court," Charlotte stated. "My only demand is the last piece of intelligence that allows me to do it. Tell me the identity of the person who provided Joseph Lomax Jr., your son and the operative, with the key to Senator Gray's highly secured townhome. That person is the deepest asset in Gray's immediate circle—the one who set up the entire operation."

Lomax stared at her, tears finally tracing clean lines through the grime of his despair. He understood the gravity of the request. This was the final betrayal of the man he was sworn to protect, the final collapse of the facade.

"The key," Lomax choked out, his voice thin and defeated. "The key was not given by an operative. It was given by the most trusted, least suspected person in the Senator's life. The man who had access to the master key safe at all times, the man who handled all of Gray's personal arrangements and security schedules."

Lomax leaned forward, his hands grasping the edge of the table, his head bowed in absolute defeat.

"It was Mr. James Fitzgerald, Ms. Reed. The Senator's personal, longtime aide. Fitzgerald had unlimited access. He was a trusted friend, part of the family for thirty years. He gave the key to my son on the night of the murder. He is the true gatekeeper of the Perseus network inside Gray's personal life."

The name landed heavily in the sterile room. Not a foreign assassin or a campaign official, but a trusted, decades-long friend. A silent, invisible gatekeeper planted thirty years ago.

Charlotte felt a cold knot tighten in her stomach. The treason was deeper and more patient than she had imagined.

"Thank you, Judge," Charlotte said, her voice now softer, recognizing the man's genuine, crippling defeat. "You have made the right choice for the country. Now, we move."

She pulled out her secure, satellite phone, typing rapidly.

To: Anne Austin (Perseus Protocol). Message: Fitzgerald. James Fitzgerald. Personal aide. Master Key. Deepest asset. Get eyes on him NOW.

Charlotte then slid the black terminal across the table to the Judge.

"Here is the laptop, Judge. Take it. Contact your son. Tell him the deal. Immunity for the murder, in exchange for exposing the network. Tell him that if he attempts to harm anyone—Wilfred Sinclair, Detective Austin, or myself—I will immediately submit the full, unredacted, and un-coerced mirror of this drive to the entire D.O.J. The choice is his. His freedom or his network."

Lomax clutched the laptop to his chest, the physical weight of his sin. He rose stiffly, looking older and smaller than any judge she had ever seen.

"And you, Ms. Reed," Lomax whispered, turning toward the door. "You will lose everything for this. Your record, your firm, your reputation. You have no idea what you've unleashed."

"I have my integrity, Judge," Charlotte said, watching him leave. "And now I have the name of the man who sold the President."

Final Tracking and the Trap (Joseph Lomax Jr.)

04:45—A Discreet Parking Garage, Bethesda, Maryland

Miles away, at the same moment his father was crumbling, Joseph Lomax Jr. was operating on pure, desperate adrenaline. He was sitting in a high-powered SUV in a dark, empty parking garage, staring at a satellite map on his dashboard.

His surveillance on Wilfred Sinclair had been broken by the theft of the *J.L. Senior* terminal. The laptop was his only reliable tracker, containing a highly sensitive GPS beacon that pinged its location every thirty seconds.

The last secure ping was 04:35 a.m., placing the terminal not at Anne Austin's home, but in the federal annex building near Foggy Bottom. His father's panic call—warning him to stand down and claiming the evidence was secured—had not swayed him. He knew his father was compromised by the very defense attorney who now held the key to his life.

The terminal is the network's command center. The theft must be neutralized immediately.

Lomax Jr. recognized the address of the annex building: it was the same discreet, forgotten tower where Senator Gray had conducted his initial, sensitive crisis meetings, the same place where Charlotte Reed had set up her defense command center.

He was being drawn into a trap, but he had no choice. The stolen terminal contained the liquidation codes for the remaining Perseus funds—funds he desperately needed to retrieve and secure before the network realized the full scale of Wilfred's theft.

He pulled out his secondary, encrypted phone. He needed a clear path to the terminal. He dialed a number he rarely used, the number of the deep asset who had been silently guarding Senator Gray for decades.

"Fitzgerald," Lomax Jr. barked into the phone. "I need eyes on the Reed office at the annex. I need to know the moment Charlotte Reed leaves that room. I'm moving in to retrieve the terminal. She has exposed us to Father."

James Fitzgerald, the Senator's devoted, silver-haired personal aide, replied with quiet, unwavering authority. "She hasn't left the room, Joey. The Judge is with her now. Give me ten minutes. I will ensure the Judge and the laptop are secured, and Miss Reed is contained. We cannot afford the exposure of this terminal."

Lomax Jr. felt a surge of professional relief. The gatekeeper was still in position. "Ten minutes, Fitzgerald. If I lose that terminal, we are both dead."

He hung up, slamming the SUV into reverse. He was heading for the annex, certain the laptop was the key to his survival. He had no idea that his father had just traded his name to Charlotte Reed, and that James Fitzgerald, the deep asset, was already working on a plan to silence both Charlotte and the Judge.

The Arraignment Clock (Charlotte Reed)

05:00—Defense Command Center, D.C.

Charlotte Reed watched the clock on the conference room wall. Lomax, Sr. was gone, having slipped back out into the pre-dawn hours to execute the recusal and attempt to contact his son.

The office door opened quietly. It was Detective Anne Austin, having used the unsecured service stairs to make her ascent. She looked pale, her arm rigid in the brace, but her eyes were alert.

"He confessed?" Anne whispered, her gaze sweeping the room.

"He confessed everything," Charlotte confirmed, her voice low. "The coercion, the five hundred thousand, the denial of our motions—all to save his son. And he gave me the name of the deepest asset in Gray's organization."

"Who?"

"James Fitzgerald. Gray's personal aide. Thirty years of access. He gave Lomax Jr. the master key to the townhome."

Anne cursed, a single, sharp exhale of realization. "Fitzgerald. The man with the complete security overview. That confirms the long-term penetration. He's the real handler."

Charlotte looked at the clock. The arraignment was approaching fast, and Fitzgerald, the handler, was still loose.

"Fitzgerald thinks the Judge is still running cover for the network," Charlotte explained. "He doesn't know Lomax has flipped. And Lomax Jr. is heading back here now, hunting the stolen terminal, not knowing his father just sold him out."

Charlotte sat down at her computer, the only clean piece of equipment in the room, and began typing the highly specific, legally devastating motion that would be the centerpiece of the arraignment.

"The deal is set, Anne. The Judge recuses, and we submit a sealed brief to the incoming, unbiased Judge detailing the initial coercion and the treasonous nature of the prosecution's timeline. Senator Gray will be cleared of the murder charge based on manufactured evidence, and the D.O.J. will open a federal case against Perseus, beginning with Joseph Lomax Jr."

Anne nodded, her eyes fixed on the door. "Then we have maybe thirty minutes until Lomax Jr. arrives here to retrieve his leverage. We need to secure the Judge before his son silences him, and we need to secure Gray before Fitzgerald moves to cut the final loose end—the Asset who knows too much."

Charlotte finished the filing, hitting the send button to the Federal Clerk's office. The motion was submitted.

She closed her laptop, her own perfect record now utterly secondary to the global stakes.

"The Judge made his choice, Anne. Now, we make ours. We separate the traitor from the asset. We go after Fitzgerald, and we get the Senator out of D.C. before the Perseus network realizes the game is over."

Charlotte stood, grabbing her briefcase. The arraignment was no longer a legal hearing; it was a distraction, a brief, noisy curtain while the real war—the war against the traitors and the assassins—was fought in the shadows of the capital.

CHAPTER 11

The Hammer Falls (Judge Lomax, Sr. & Joseph Lomax Jr.)

05:05—Georgetown Townhome District, D.C.

Judge Joseph Lomax, Sr. stumbled through the front door of his Georgetown apartment, clutching the black laptop like a shield against the coming storm. The weight of the terminal was nothing compared to the crushing burden of the name he had just uttered: James Fitzgerald. Thirty years of trust, thirty years of political infrastructure, all sold out for the life of his criminal son.

He dropped the laptop onto his kitchen counter, his hands shaking so violently he could barely press the power button. He was not just a traitor; he was a desperate father, clinging to the impossible deal Charlotte Reed had offered: immunity from murder in exchange for exposing treason.

The terminal booted up, and Lomax immediately located the secure application that connected to his son's untraceable phone line. He had to reach Joseph before the boy reached Charlotte's office, before the rage of the network consumed them all.

He initiated the call, his heart hammering against his ribs, a frantic rhythm of paternal fear.

The phone rang three times. Then, a low, smooth voice answered. It wasn't Joseph.

"Hello, Father."

The voice was cultured, calm, and utterly chilling in its lack of surprise. It was Joseph Lomax Jr., the operative, already anticipating his father's call.

"Joey, thank God. Listen to me. You have to stand down. Now. I've secured the terminal, and I've made a deal with Reed. You walk free, son. You walk free from the murder charge, but you have to give them the network. It's over. Phase One Retrieval is off. You're exposed."

Silence stretched across the line, heavy with implication. Lomax Sr. could hear the faint, high-pitched whine of an engine in the background—Joseph was in the vehicle, moving fast.

"You met with her, Father," Joseph Jr.'s voice was flat, laced with a profound, terrifying disappointment. "You went to the federal annex. Fitzgerald told me you were going to secure the laptop. He told me you were contained. But you flipped. You traded me."

"I saved you, Joseph! I secured you immunity from the murder! They want the network, not the son. You cooperate, and you live! You will be free of them!"

A harsh, metallic sound, like a safety being released, clicked on the other end of the line.

"I was never *free* of them, Father," Joseph Jr. said, his voice now dangerously soft. "The network is my life. The mission is my life. You don't understand. This isn't a mob boss we're dealing with; this is the slow installation of a puppet President.

You have ruined decades of work and exposed our deepest asset."

"Who? Fitzgerald? He was the key. I gave his name to Reed! That was the deal!"

"Fitzgerald is the *gatekeeper*, Father. He's the man who ensures access. But I am the asset that was created to protect the *primary asset*—Senator Gray. My life was engineered to be your pressure point. And now, you've broken. You've exposed the Judge, the operative, and the gatekeeper. You have failed the mission, and you have destroyed the final leverage point of the network."

Joseph Jr.'s voice tightened into a cold, ruthless snarl. "The deal is nullified, Father. The network doesn't negotiate with enemies, and you are now the primary threat. You are the only person who knows that I have the power to destroy the entire network from within. Containment Protocol is now active. I am less than five minutes from the annex. I will retrieve the terminal, and I will eliminate the two primary targets: Charlotte Reed and Detective Anne Austin."

The line went dead.

Judge Lomax, Sr. stood paralyzed in his kitchen, the cold realization sinking into his bones. He hadn't bought his son's freedom; he had signed his son's death warrant, his own, and Charlotte Reed's. The deal was a lie. Joseph Jr. was not a coerced victim; he was a fanatic. And he was hunting.

Lomax knew his next move would be his last. He had to warn Charlotte. He had to protect the only person who could still expose the treason. He grabbed the laptop, not to use it, but to destroy it. He found a hammer in a utility drawer and smashed the hard drive with a single, furious blow, shattering the logic board. The evidence of his coercion was gone, but so was the Judge's leverage over his son.

He then stumbled to his secure phone, dialing Charlotte Reed's private, off-the-record number, praying she hadn't left the office.

The Escape Hatch (Charlotte Reed & Anne Austin)

05:10—Defense Command Center, D.C.

Charlotte Reed and Detective Anne Austin were already moving. Anne, despite the crippling pain in her arm, had used the annex's architectural diagrams (sourced by Elias Vance hours before) to map their escape route.

"The Judge is compromised, Charlotte, but he's not the target anymore," Anne said, holding the fractured arm close to her chest. "Lomax Jr. is heading here for the laptop. He won't use the main lobby; he'll use the service entrance near the fire escape."

Charlotte was mirroring the contents of the *J.L. Senior* terminal onto a secure, encrypted flash drive—the one she was submitting to the D.O.J. as her guarantee. She worked with manic speed, watching the progress bar crawl across her screen.

"I have the mirror image. It's submitting now to my external server," Charlotte confirmed, pulling the drive out. "This is the only copy. If Lomax Jr. gets the original terminal, we lose the liquidation codes Wilfred stole, but we still have the leverage of Lomax Sr.'s coercion."

The satellite phone on the desk rang, its emergency ring a jarring, violent sound in the pre-dawn quiet. The caller ID was JUDGE LOMAX SR - PRIVATE.

Charlotte immediately answered, placing the call on speaker. "Judge, what is it?"

Lomax's voice was ragged, desperate, filled with the static of absolute terror. "Reed! Listen to me! He's coming! Joseph is a fanatic! He didn't flip! He's five minutes out! He thinks you have the terminal! He's running Containment Protocol! You have to get out now! He said he's eliminating *you and the detective*! And I told him Fitzgerald was the key, Reed! I told him everything! I've doomed us all!"

The line broke off with a final, echoing crash—the sound of the Judge's phone being smashed against a counter.

Charlotte locked eyes with Anne. The immediate threat was no longer an impersonal shadow; it was a deadly, professional executioner five minutes away.

"He knows we know Fitzgerald's name," Charlotte said, grabbing her briefcase. "That makes us, and the Senator, obsolete and immediate liabilities. We need to go."

Anne was already at the fire escape door, checking the latch. "Lomax Jr. will hit the service entrance first. The minute he realizes the terminal is gone, he'll sweep the entire floor. We go down the fire escape to the service tunnel. It connects to the abandoned metro line under the annex. Elias is waiting for us with a car on the surface ten blocks from here."

The air in the room suddenly changed—a sudden, subtle shift in pressure against the closed office door. Someone was trying the external lock.

"Too late," Anne whispered, drawing her gun with her left hand, the fractured arm dangling uselessly at her side. "He's here. Front door first, then the fire escape."

Charlotte didn't panic. She moved to the side of the room, near the internal wall. "You can't take him, Anne. He's tactical, and you're one-handed. We need a diversion."

She grabbed the empty gym bag Anne had used for the drop-off and shoved a stack of thick legal binders inside. She then used a small, powerful magnet from her briefcase and quickly taped it to the bag's lining.

Charlotte slid the gym bag under the desk, near the main entrance. "The original terminal is gone. The GPS beacon on the terminal has stopped pinging, which Lomax Jr. will have noticed. But he's running on instinct and rage. He'll be looking for any residual magnetic signature—anything that suggests the terminal was just moved or transferred."

Anne understood immediately. "The magnet will create a localized electromagnetic surge that fools his internal sensors into thinking the terminal is still in the room, under the desk."

"Exactly. It gives us maybe thirty seconds of distraction," Charlotte confirmed.

The external door lock began to click, slowly, methodically, not with a key, but with a highly specialized hacking tool.

"Now!" Anne hissed.

Charlotte dashed to the fire escape door, Anne throwing the heavy metal latch open. The cold, damp air from the stairwell rushed in.

They plunged out onto the grated metal steps. Behind them, the main office door crashed inward with a violent, splintering sound.

Joseph Lomax Jr. stood in the doorway. His eyes, sweeping the empty room, were blazing with cold fury. He saw the fire escape door swinging shut. He moved instantly, sprinting across the office, ready to pursue.

But as he ran past the desk, his internal sensor screamed a warning: TARGET COLD. STRONG RESIDUAL MAGNETIC SIGNATURE DETECTED. LOCATION: UNDER DESK.

Lomax Jr. swore violently. He didn't hesitate. He dropped to his knees, ripping the fake gym bag out from under the desk. He tore the bag open, pulling out the worthless binders, his face a mask of absolute, professional rage.

The delay was precisely twenty-five seconds.

By the time Lomax Jr. realized the deception, Charlotte and Anne were already three flights down, reaching the access point for the sub-level service tunnel.

The Race to the Asset (Anne Austin & Charlotte Reed)

05:25—Abandoned D.C. Metro Line, Beneath Foggy Bottom

Anne and Charlotte ran, their footsteps echoing eerily in the dark, cavernous tunnel, using Anne's tactical flashlight to navigate the dusty tracks. Elias Vance met them where the service tunnel connected to the old, decommissioned metro line.

"Lomax Jr. will be on the surface in sixty seconds," Elias stated, his face grim. "He knows the layout of these tunnels from his campaign security work. He will intercept the car."

"He has the terminal, but I have the mirror image drive," Charlotte confirmed, shoving the tiny flash drive into Elias's hands. "Lomax Sr. confessed. The deepest asset is James Fitzgerald—Senator Gray's personal aide. He's the gatekeeper. Fitzgerald thinks the Judge and I are still contained, but he is now exposed. He will move immediately to silence the Senator—the compromised asset—before the arraignment. Senator Gray is sequestered in the luxury suite at the Embassy Suites downtown. We have to get to him first."

"The Embassy Suites is a known campaign safe house," Elias said, already running the coordinates. "Fitzgerald will assume Gray is still there. If he's the deep asset, he has access codes. He can be in Gray's room in fifteen minutes."

"Fitzgerald just talked to Lomax Jr., telling him the Judge and I were contained," Charlotte said, strapping herself into the passenger seat of Elias's modified escape car. "He knows the entire operation is collapsing. His primary directive will be to neutralize the Asset and disappear. We have fifteen minutes to extract the Senator."

The car screamed through the dark, deserted tunnels of the old metro line—an illegal, dangerous shortcut that put them beneath the rush-hour traffic.

The Final Betrayal (James Fitzgerald)

05:40—Embassy Suites Luxury Suite, Downtown D.C.

James Fitzgerald looked like the perfect picture of presidential devotion: silver-haired, impeccably tailored, and possessing the calm, reassuring demeanor of a man who managed the world's most powerful people. He stood outside Senator Marcus David Gray's sequestered suite, holding a tray with a bottle of mineral water and two protein bars.

He had just received a furious, coded message from Joseph Lomax Jr.

Containment Protocol Failure. Father has flipped. Reed has the terminal. Fitzgerald, you are the final Asset. Eliminate the Asset (Gray) before the recusal is filed. Initiate immediate Egress.

Fitzgerald, the trusted aide of thirty years, felt a cold, professional calm settle over him. He was the Gatekeeper. He was the one who had spent decades placing the Asset in position. His life's work could not be undone by a rogue detective and a clever defense attorney. The mission was paramount.

He used his personal security override key to bypass the suite's primary locks, slipping silently into the opulent room.

Senator Gray was asleep on the couch, exhausted by the stress and the constant surveillance.

Fitzgerald placed the tray on the coffee table. He reached inside his jacket, retrieving a small, specialized syringe filled with a clear, fast-acting neurotoxin—the same type of agent Lomax Jr. had used to incapacitate Sarah Jenkins. He had manufactured it himself years ago, intended as a final solution for compromised assets.

He approached the sleeping Senator, the needle aimed for the soft skin of Gray's neck.

"Forgive me, Marcus," Fitzgerald whispered, the only flicker of genuine human emotion in his voice. "You were a magnificent Asset, but you've become a liability. The mission must continue."

He heard the faint, metallic click of the suite's second, heavy-duty security lock being picked, then the rapid whisper of hushed, urgent voices outside the door.

"Too late," Anne Austin's voice hissed outside. "He's still inside. Get ready."

Fitzgerald swore under his breath. Charlotte Reed and the detective. They were faster than the security protocols had allowed for. They had beat Lomax Jr.'s containment sweep.

He quickly pocketed the syringe. He couldn't risk a lethal injection with them outside the door; the police would be called instantly. He needed a distraction.

Fitzgerald moved to the sliding glass door of the suite, which opened onto a small, private terrace overlooking the city.

The Rooftop Gambit (Charlotte Reed & Anne Austin)

05:45—Embassy Suites Suite, Downtown D.C.

Charlotte Reed kicked the suite door inward, Anne Austin rushing in behind her, gun raised.

"Police! Freeze, Fitzgerald!" Anne yelled, her voice hoarse.

Fitzgerald was already on the terrace, grabbing the Senator's luggage—a single, black, rolling briefcase—and throwing it over the railing onto the roof of the adjacent parking garage three stories below.

"He's destroying evidence!" Charlotte yelled, running onto the terrace.

Fitzgerald turned, his face calm, terrifyingly devoid of panic. "The Asset is safe for now, Ms. Reed. But the mission continues."

He vaulted over the low railing, landing on the narrow ledge of the building's exterior façade.

"He's escaping! He's going to use the exterior maintenance ladder to get to the roof!" Anne screamed, running to the railing.

Charlotte grabbed Anne's arm, forcing her to stop. "No, Anne! He's the gatekeeper! If he escapes, we lose the highest-value asset. We go through the suite. Get the Senator!"

Charlotte ran to the sleeping Senator, checking his pulse. He was alive, just heavily sedated. She knew the police could not be called; they would expose the entire conspiracy and compromise the D.O.J. investigation before it even started.

"Senator Gray!" Charlotte slapped him hard, forcing him toward consciousness. "Wake up! You are in extreme danger!

Your aide, Fitzgerald, is the deep asset! He just tried to kill you!"

Gray stirred, his eyes cloudy. "Fitzgerald? What... what are you saying, Charlotte?"

"He's the one who gave the key to the killer. He is the treason. Anne, get the Senator up! We go now! We go to Elias's secure location!"

Anne, guarding the door, realized the gravity of the situation. Fitzgerald wasn't a hitman; he was the head of security for the network. He had just thrown the Asset's briefcase—which likely contained his final set of campaign funding and contacts—onto the adjacent roof.

"We need the Senator's briefcase, Charlotte! It contains the final piece of the financial map! It's on the garage roof!" Anne yelled.

Charlotte looked at the terrified Senator, then at the railing. The sun was now a sliver of violent red on the horizon. The arraignment was approaching. Lomax Jr. was closing in. Fitzgerald was on the loose.

"Anne, you extract the Senator. Use the service elevator and get to Elias. I'm retrieving the evidence."

Before Anne could object, Charlotte had grabbed the Senator's key card and was vaulting over the low railing, using the same precarious ledge Fitzgerald had just used. She was a lawyer, not a field operative, but the absolute need to retrieve the final piece of evidence—the financial map that connected Gray to the Belgrade money—overrode all sense of safety.

She ran along the narrow, three-story-high ledge, her heels slipping on the damp metal. She could see the black briefcase resting on the smooth tar surface of the parking garage roof just a few feet away.

She made the jump, landing hard on the roof. The impact jarred her entire body, but she was up in a second, sprinting for the briefcase.

She grabbed the handle, spinning around, only to find Joseph Lomax Jr. standing ten feet away, his face contorted in a mask of absolute hatred, a silenced pistol raised and aimed directly at her chest.

Lomax Jr. had missed the Senator, but he had found the Asset's lawyer and the final piece of evidence.

"The terminal is corrupted, Reed," Lomax Jr. snarled, his voice a low hiss. "But the briefcase remains. The network is secured. You have no move left."

Charlotte, trapped, clutching the Senator's briefcase, looked up. She saw the flash of the rising sun reflecting off the sniper scope of a weapon aimed at Lomax Jr. from the adjacent building—the signal of Anne Austin's secret backup, Elias Vance, coming to her rescue.

But the shot wasn't fired. Elias couldn't risk hitting Charlotte.

Charlotte had one second left. She didn't drop the case. She threw it, hard and low, directly at Lomax Jr.'s knees.

The hit was solid. Lomax Jr. cried out in pain, the shot from his silenced pistol going high and wide, shattering a window on the building behind them.

The impact bought Charlotte the precious second she needed. She sprinted toward the far side of the roof, away from the operative, toward the edge where the maintenance stairs led down to the street.

Lomax Jr. recovered quickly, sighting his weapon again.

He fired two shots. The first tore through the sleeve of Charlotte's jacket. The second was deadly accurate, slamming into the briefcase and sending sparks and metal fragments flying. The briefcase, containing the final financial ledgers, was destroyed.

Charlotte didn't stop. She dove down the maintenance stairs, leaving the wreckage of the briefcase—and the final piece of financial evidence—behind her. She had saved the Senator, she had broken the Judge, but she had lost the final ledger.

The game was now played on a new field, with the Asset safe, the Judge recused, and the final Asset, Fitzgerald, on the loose. The Arraignment was only hours away, and the court would now meet a new, uncompromised judge, ready to receive Charlotte Reed's devastating, treasonous motion.

CHAPTER 12

The New Bench (Rupert McCallister & Georgia Wright)

07:30—District Courtroom 302, D.C.

The chaos was palpable, a dense, electric hum of rumor and anxiety that had nothing to do with justice and everything to do with power. The media swarm outside was unprecedented, the cameras trained on every vehicle that pulled up to the Federal Annex, waiting for the arrival of the presidential hopeful, Senator Marcus David Gray, for his highly anticipated murder arraignment.

Inside Courtroom 302, the atmosphere was a mix of tension and bewilderment. The prosecution team, led by Georgia Wright, looked tight and nervous, whispering furiously at their table. At the defense table, Rupert McCallister sat alone, meticulously stacking Charlotte Reed's legal pads, his face a perfect mask of aristocratic calm that belied his racing pulse.

Charlotte was absent. Senator Gray was absent. And the biggest shock of the morning was the absence of the presiding Judge.

A grim-faced court clerk announced the proceedings. "All rise. The Honorable Judge Joseph Lomax, Sr, has filed an immediate, voluntary recusal from this case, citing an unavoidable, undisclosed personal necessity. Presiding over the arraignment and all subsequent motions will be The Honorable Judge Helena Vance."

A collective gasp swept through the gallery. The move was instantaneous, unprecedented, and, to everyone present, inexplicable. Judge Lomax, the formidable, veteran jurist, had voluntarily abandoned the highest-profile trial in the nation's capital, citing *personal necessity* rather than a legal conflict.

A tall, severe woman with steel-gray hair and an expression that promised zero tolerance for theatrics swept onto the bench. Judge Helena Vance was known for her brilliance, her impenetrable objectivity, and her absolute disdain for political maneuvering. She was the polar opposite of the compromised man Charlotte had just blackmailed into retreat.

Georgia Wright immediately rose, her voice tight with fury and barely concealed fear. She had spent the early morning hours absorbing the shock of Lomax's retreat, knowing instantly that this meant Charlotte Reed had found the leverage. Lomax hadn't just recused; he had flipped the table on the entire *Perseus* operation.

"Your Honor, the State objects to the sudden, late-hour recusal of Judge Lomax," Georgia announced, choosing her words carefully. She couldn't mention the treason, but she had to delay the inevitable. "The integrity of the case requires immediate explanation for this move, which the State suspects is based on highly irregular contact from the defense team."

Judge Vance leaned forward, her gaze cutting into Georgia Wright. "The objection is noted, Ms. Wright, and it is overruled. Judge Lomax's recusal is effective immediately. He is no longer a factor in this Court. I have been appointed to preside, and I will be guided solely by the law and the facts before me, not by speculation regarding the prior Judge's personal affairs."

She shifted her gaze to Rupert McCallister. "Mr. McCallister, where is your client, and where is lead counsel, Ms. Reed? The time for the arraignment is now."

Rupert rose, embodying the cool, detached confidence Charlotte had instilled in him. "Your Honor, my client, Senator Gray, is in secure transit. He will appear for the formal plea of *Not Guilty* when a new, uncompromised Judge can review the sensitive nature of our pending emergency motion. As for Ms. Reed, she is finalizing the submission of a sealed, ex parte motion to this Court, which has a direct and immediate bearing on the integrity of the prosecution's entire case."

Georgia Wright pounded her fist on the table. "A sealed motion? This is outrageous obstruction, Your Honor! They are delaying the arraignment to avoid entering a plea! We demand the motion be revealed and dismissed as grounds for contempt!"

Judge Vance held up a single, imperious hand, silencing Georgia. She looked down at the documents before her. "The Court is in receipt of a sealed envelope, filed precisely at 06:00 a.m. this morning by Ms. Reed. This motion, entitled Motion for Judicial Integrity and Expository Discovery, is now unsealed for the Court's immediate review."

She opened the thick, legal document Charlotte had filed hours before her narrow escape from Lomax Jr.

The room fell into an agonizing silence as Judge Vance read the motion. Charlotte had not accused Judge Lomax of treason directly; she had laid out the legal logic of the coercion. She detailed the *Mirza concession*—the admission that the victim may have been incapacitated—followed by the *Lomax recusal*, and finally, requested an order compelling the D.O.J. to initiate an immediate Counter-Intelligence Investigation based on credible evidence that the murder charge was manufactured by a foreign power to leverage a sitting Federal Judge and conceal the identity of the Primary Asset (Senator Gray).

Judge Vance finished reading. She placed the document down slowly, her expression unreadable.

"Ms. Wright," the Judge said, her voice dangerously quiet. "The Defense is formally alleging that the murder charge against Senator Gray is based on manufactured evidence, designed as part of a treasonous plot to compromise the Bench and install a foreign asset. Ms. Reed has submitted evidence of coercion. Do you have any immediate, exculpatory evidence or testimony that would immediately discredit these grave allegations?"

Georgia Wright looked around desperately, her mind racing. She knew Lomax had flipped. She knew the network was compromised. She had been tasked with a simple murder case, and now she was facing a treason charge based on her association with the corrupt Judge. She was trapped between the legal consequences of the truth and the physical consequences of the network.

"Your Honor, the State has conclusive DNA evidence linking Senator Gray to the victim at the time of death! The entire motion is a paranoid fiction designed to create a political defense!"

"But you have no evidence to contradict the former Medical Examiner's concession that the victim may have been pre-incapacitated, which destroys the struggle narrative," Judge Vance pointed out coolly. "Furthermore, you have no explanation for the abrupt recusal of the presiding Judge just hours before the arraignment, following a private, undocumented meeting with lead defense counsel."

Judge Vance looked at the clock. The arraignment was hours overdue. The nation was watching. She had to act with decisive authority.

"The Court recognizes the extraordinary nature of this motion and the severity of the allegations," Judge Vance declared. "Given the recusal of the previous Judge, the plausible compromise of the evidence timeline as established by the Mirza testimony, and the credible, sealed evidence of coercion now before the Court, I cannot in good conscience allow the arraignment to proceed on the current indictment."

She struck the gavel hard, the sound echoing through the stunned courtroom.

"The Court hereby staying the arraignment indefinitely and issuing an immediate Order for Judicial Inquiry. I am compelling the D.O.J.'s Counter-Intelligence Division to seize all evidence and communications related to former Judge Joseph Lomax, Sr, and Assistant District Attorney Georgia Wright, pending a full, non-political investigation into the allegations raised by the Defense. This murder case is no longer a local criminal matter; it is a Federal National Security Inquiry."

Georgia Wright collapsed into her chair, her face draining of color. She was under federal investigation, her career instantly destroyed, all because the 21st Juror had been broken by Charlotte Reed.

Rupert McCallister let out a slow, controlled exhale of relief. The arraignment was stopped. The D.O.J. was in. Charlotte had won the first, crucial battle.

The Sanctuary and the Scraps (Charlotte Reed & Anne Austin)

08:45—Elias Vance's Secure Location, Virginia

Charlotte Reed sat on a leather sofa in Elias Vance's highly secured safe house—a discreet, underground command center beneath a rural horse farm in Virginia. She was drinking black coffee, her adrenaline finally settling into a deep, bone-weary exhaustion.

Senator Marcus David Gray was in the next room, talking nervously to Anne Austin. The Senator was panicked, having finally been informed by Charlotte that his longtime, trusted aide, James Fitzgerald, had tried to murder him hours ago.

"We need to bring Fitzgerald in immediately," Gray insisted, rubbing his temples. "He was like a brother to me. I need to know why he betrayed me."

"Because you were a liability to the network that installed you, Senator," Anne said, her voice firm. She had applied a professional bandage to her fractured arm and was now focused entirely on the intelligence war. "Fitzgerald is not a brother; he's a deep asset who's been protecting the campaign's true purpose—your ascension to the presidency—for decades. He is the Gatekeeper. He knows every password, every security flaw, and every contact point."

Charlotte walked in, placing her empty mug down. "Fitzgerald is not interested in talking, Senator. He's interested in neutralizing the final threat: the mirror image of your former Judge's terminal, which contains the evidence of your coercion."

She looked at Anne. "The arraignment is stayed. Judge Vance has ordered a D.O.J. inquiry into the Judge and the ADA. We are officially in the federal intelligence game now. But we have a major problem: Fitzgerald knows Lomax Jr. failed to retrieve the terminal, and he knows Lomax Jr. destroyed your briefcase. He knows that the only remaining leverage is the flash drive Elias has."

Elias Vance emerged from his server room, holding the tiny flash drive in a clear, sealed evidence bag. "This is the only copy of the drive I managed to mirror from Lomax Sr.'s personal terminal. It contains the evidence of the Judge's coercion, the memo confirming Perseus Protocol was active, and Lomax Jr.'s security schematics for the campaign. It's our insurance, Charlotte. It's the proof we need to force the D.O.J. to charge treason against the entire network."

"But we lost the financial ledger," Charlotte countered, thinking of the shots that destroyed the briefcase. "The final piece of the financial map—the documents that tied Gray's personal wealth to the Belgrade money after Wilfred fled—is gone. We can prove Lomax was compromised, but we can't prove *Gray was knowingly compromised* without the ledger."

Senator Gray looked horrified. "I swear, Charlotte, I never knew about any of this. I thought Fitzgerald was just managing the PAC money."

"He was managing a shadow government, Senator," Charlotte said, her eyes relentless. "And now we need to anticipate his next move. Fitzgerald is the ultimate insider. He knows every loophole, every blind spot, and every person who owes the campaign a favor. He knows Elias is the only person who could have cracked the Judge's terminal."

Charlotte turned to Elias. "Fitzgerald will not hunt me or Anne. We are too exposed. He will hunt the drive. And he knows exactly who you are, Elias. Your background as a former FBI cyber analyst is public record. He knows you are the only person Charlotte Reed would trust with evidence this explosive."

"He'll target my infrastructure," Elias agreed, his face grim. "Not my person. He'll find the physical location of my most secured server bank—the one that holds this drive."

The Gatekeeper's Bait (James Fitzgerald)

10:00—The Executive Office Building, White House Complex

James Fitzgerald sat in a secured, private office within the Executive Office Building, calmly reviewing the immediate, devastating fallout from the Lomax recusal. He was not panicked; he was focused. The Judge's flip was an annoyance, a loss of control, but not a defeat.

He had ditched the neurotoxin and his primary escape vehicle, and he was now back at the heart of the capital, using his deep political contacts to initiate his counter-plan.

He received a cryptic, encrypted message confirming the Judge's full confession to Charlotte, including the fact that he named Fitzgerald as the Gatekeeper.

They know my name, Fitzgerald thought, a cold, clinical acceptance settling over him. *And they have the terminal data.*

He looked at the security monitoring software running on his laptop. He was now running the full sweep on all of Elias Vance's registered assets, knowing the former FBI analyst was the only person Charlotte Reed would rely on to secure the mirror-image drive.

Fitzgerald's political connections ran deeper than the campaign. He was the Gatekeeper because he had spent thirty years cultivating loyalty at the highest levels of the D.C. infrastructure.

He picked up a white, secure phone—a phone reserved for the most sensitive communication—and dialed the private number of Senator William Cross, the current chairman of the Senate Intelligence Committee.

Cross answered immediately. "Fitzgerald. What in God's name is happening with Gray? Lomax recused! The entire city is collapsing."

"Senator, the campaign is under attack by a rogue element—a highly sophisticated, foreign-funded group attempting to blackmail Judge Lomax and destabilize the election. This rogue group has stolen highly classified campaign security data, and they are using a former FBI analyst to process it. His name is Elias Vance."

Fitzgerald knew exactly how to frame the lie: counter-terrorism.

"I need you to use your influence on the Intelligence Committee to get me the physical location of Elias Vance's primary data storage facility. He is running high-level decryption on stolen D.O.D. files—a breach of national security. Get me the location now, Senator. I am the only one who can retrieve this data before it falls into enemy hands."

Senator Cross, terrified by the mention of D.O.D. files and foreign-funded blackmail, immediately agreed to leverage his contacts in the FBI's legal team to pinpoint Vance's most secure facility.

Fitzgerald hung up. He knew Vance had at least three facilities. But only one—the one he thought was impenetrable—would hold the mirror-image drive.

He looked at his watch. The game had shifted from defense to offense. He had the Senator hunting his target for him, all while Charlotte Reed thought he was on the run.

The Security Breach (Elias Vance)

12:00—Elias Vance's Secure Data Facility, Sterling, Virginia

The facility was a masterpiece of paranoia: a windowless,

concrete bunker disguised as a suburban warehouse, protected by three layers of bio-metric locks and a dedicated, redundant power grid. Inside, Elias Vance sat in the cold silence of his server room, the *J.L. Senior* mirror-image drive resting in a cradle connected to a server running a seven-layer encryption loop.

He was running a full analysis of the drive, looking for anything Charlotte and Anne had missed. He had found something disturbing: a repeating, encrypted signature in the drive's communication logs that wasn't related to the Judge, the son, or the campaign. It was an intermittent, highly specific ping—a heartbeat signal.

"It's a secondary asset beacon," Elias muttered to himself, tracing the ping's origin to an untraceable satellite line. *"A clean-up crew. The network knows the terminal is gone, but they want to know where it is."*

The ping's frequency was accelerating. The network was closing in.

Elias immediately initiated the "Blackout Protocol"—a systemic shutdown of all external communication from the facility. He locked the drive in a specialized, titanium safe embedded in the concrete floor. He then set up a final, lethal defensive measure: a high-voltage, non-lethal electrical charge running through the facility's exterior perimeter fence, designed to disable any intruder attempting a forced entry.

Just as he finished the final lockdown sequence, his phone rang. It was an encrypted number he didn't recognize. He answered cautiously.

"Elias Vance. You are under arrest for the possession of stolen federal and D.O.D. files," a voice commanded, severe and military. "You have breached national security. We have the facility surrounded. Open the doors immediately, or we will breach the site with force."

Elias checked his external monitoring feed. There were no marked cars. But there were four massive, black SUVs parked discreetly down the road, men in dark, tactical gear standing near the perimeter. They weren't D.O.J. or FBI. They were private security contractors, run by the kind of firm that worked for foreign intelligence or political black ops. Fitzgerald had found him.

Elias grabbed a tactical shotgun he kept locked in a secure cabinet. He ran to the main server rack, pulling the main circuit breaker. The lights flickered, throwing the room into emergency low power.

"You won't breach," Elias whispered into the phone, his voice laced with venom. "This drive holds proof of treason against a sitting Federal Judge, and the man you work for is the operative who assassinated Sarah Jenkins. I am not opening this door."

He hung up, running to the exterior monitoring station. The tactical team—Fitzgerald's clean-up crew—were already approaching the perimeter fence.

They reached the fence, and the lead man, a massive figure with a military build, placed a hand on the wire. The instant his skin touched the high-voltage wire, a blinding blue arc of electricity exploded. The man screamed, collapsing instantly.

"Static perimeter is hot!" the second operative yelled into his comms.

The delay was brief, but critical. Elias had bought himself seconds. He ran to the loading dock, realizing the entire facility was a trap. He could not fight four trained assassins, and he could not let them take the mirror-image drive.

He had one last move: the final detonation sequence. A localized, controlled explosion designed to destroy the entire server bank and the titanium safe containing the drive, ensuring the evidence would never fall into the wrong hands.

He placed his hand on the final, shielded panel of the server rack, ready to activate the sequence.

A high-pitched, insistent *thunk* sounded against the metal wall of the loading dock—the sound of a breach charge being placed on the rear door.

Elias braced himself. The door would blow in three seconds. He had to decide: detonate the evidence and destroy the truth forever, or fight for the chance to save it.

The Intercept (James Fitzgerald)

13:00—Elias Vance's Secure Data Facility, Sterling, Virginia

Fitzgerald watched the surveillance feed on his tablet from the safety of his SUV. The blast from the fence was a setback, but the breach charge on the rear door would negate the perimeter.

"Go! Go! Go!" Fitzgerald commanded into his encrypted comms. "Retrieve the drive! Do not harm Vance unless absolutely necessary!"

The rear door blew inward with a concussive blast, tearing the reinforced steel off its hinges. Three tactical operatives flooded the loading dock, weapons raised.

Elias Vance was ready. He hadn't detonated the drive. He had chosen to fight for the truth.

He fired the shotgun—a non-lethal, high-density beanbag round—directly at the first operative, slamming the man backward into the concrete wall, shattering his armor and stunning him instantly.

The second operative returned fire with a suppressed weapon. Elias dove behind a stack of hard drives, the bullets tearing into the metal casing, sending sparks flying.

Fitzgerald, watching the feed, swore under his breath. Vance was smarter than he looked.

"Vance is armed and hostile! Retrieve the drive! Priority is the titanium safe on the server floor!"

Elias, using the low light and the chaotic echoes of the bunker, ran for the server room, weaving through the cold aisles of hardware. He knew he couldn't win the firefight, but he could buy time. He reached the safe, typing in the code.

The safe door opened. He grabbed the small, vital flash drive containing the mirror-image evidence, placing it in a separate, inconspicuous security pouch hidden in his fleece jacket. He then grabbed a decoy drive—a junk drive containing a complex virus—and placed it back in the safe.

The operatives burst into the server room.

"Freeze, Vance! Drop the weapon!"

Elias dropped the shotgun, raising his hands in surrender, allowing the operatives to swarm him. They slammed him onto the cold floor, searching him immediately.

"He's clean, sir! No primary drive!" the lead operative yelled into his comms.

Fitzgerald's voice crackled through the comms. "Check the safe! The drive is in the titanium safe!"

The operative rushed to the safe, grabbing the decoy drive. He held it up triumphantly.

"Target secured, sir! Mirror drive retrieved!"

"Excellent," Fitzgerald said, a cold, satisfied smile touching his lips. "Egress. Neutralize Vance and detonate the facility. Make it look like a tragic accident involving an accidental power surge."

The operative raised his weapon, aiming directly at Elias Vance's head.

Just as the operative pulled the trigger, a flash of movement exploded into the server room.

Detective Anne Austin, moving with a desperate, one-armed fury, smashed through the floor-to-ceiling glass observation window of the server room, using a heavy oxygen tank as a battering ram. The glass exploded outward, showering the room in blinding shards.

Anne landed hard, rolling immediately to her feet. The operative was stunned by the sudden, chaotic entrance. The shot meant for Elias went wide.

Anne, screaming in pain from her fractured arm, used the momentum to slam the heavy oxygen tank directly into the operative's head, knocking him unconscious instantly.

The remaining operatives turned, raising their weapons. But the sudden, illegal intervention had done its job. The facility was compromised, and the clean-up team was exposed.

Anne stood over Elias, the fragmented glass reflecting the raw determination in her eyes. "Fitzgerald wanted an accident, Elias. Let's give him one."

She grabbed the operative's discarded weapon and began firing suppressed rounds into the facility's main circuit board, initiating the self-destruct sequence. The massive server rack began to whine, its lights flashing red. The building was going into meltdown.

"Grab the drive and let's go! Now!" Anne yelled, pulling the stunned Elias to his feet.

They ran, leaving the decoy drive and the unconscious operatives inside the collapsing data center, knowing that Fitzgerald would soon realize his success was a brilliant, explosive failure. The mirror drive, the true key to the conspiracy, was safe. The Arraignment was stayed, but the war for the presidency had just escalated into an open, violent conflict.

CHAPTER 13

The Asset's Defection (Fitzgerald & Charlotte Reed)

13:15—Elias Vance's Secure Data Facility, Sterling, Virginia

The roar of the explosion was still echoing in the distance when James Fitzgerald slammed his fist against the steering wheel of his SUV. The heat from the collapsing data center was visible in the rearview camera, a massive, roiling cloud of black smoke and incandescent energy rising into the afternoon sky.

He had won. The physical drive was destroyed.

"Report!" Fitzgerald barked into his encrypted comms channel.

The lead operative's voice, raw and panicked, crackled through the speaker. "Facility is in full meltdown, sir! Internal servers detonated. Three men down, severe burns, but secured the primary drive—wait! It's the wrong drive, sir! It's a clean unit, encrypted with a heavy virus. The data is gone! And Detective Austin was here! She and Vance escaped with the evidence!"

Fitzgerald closed his eyes, his perfect, silver-haired composure dissolving into a silent, lethal rage. The entire sequence—the electrical fence, the controlled internal fire, the decoy drive in the safe—was a masterwork of defensive planning. Elias Vance had played him, turning his own clean-up operation into an explosive, costly failure. Fitzgerald, the architect of a decades-long political insertion, had been outmaneuvered by a rogue detective with a broken arm and a paranoid former analyst.

The mirror drive, containing the Judge's coercion data and the Perseus Protocol memo, was still intact. Worse, Detective Anne Austin, who had nearly been silenced twice, was alive and actively moving with the evidence.

Containment Protocol Failure. Final Egress is now required.

Fitzgerald understood the brutal mathematics of the situation. The D.O.J. inquiry, compelled by Judge Vance, was now officially active. Charlotte Reed and her team had the proof of the Judge's treason, but they lacked the final, crucial link—the financial ledger that proved Senator Marcus David Gray was a willing, knowing asset of the Belgrade network. The briefcase containing that ledger had been destroyed by Lomax Jr.

His mission was simple: Eliminate the final witness. Senator Gray, the primary asset, had become too dangerous. He knew Fitzgerald's identity and had witnessed the attempt on his life. Gray had to be silenced before Charlotte Reed could turn him into a witness for the D.O.J.

Fitzgerald grabbed his secondary, burner phone. He needed to coordinate with the only remaining active asset in the city: Joseph Lomax Jr. The last time they spoke, Lomax Jr. was heading to the Federal Annex to retrieve the *J.L. Senior* terminal. He had failed and likely realized his father had sold him out.

He typed a coded message: *JUNIOR: Egress now. Failure to secure terminal. Eliminate Asset GRAY. Location: Safe House*

Virginia. Use Asset Tracker 1.

He waited, the engine idling, watching the smoke plume. If Lomax Jr. was still operational, he would receive the order. Fitzgerald had one hour to disappear before the FBI tracked the location of the exploding data center back to his shell corporation and the security contractors he used. He shed his suit jacket, pulling on a non-descript, dark blue hoodie, preparing to dissolve into the anonymity of the D.C. suburbs.

14:30—Elias Vance's Secure Location, Virginia

The safe house was a place of quiet, sterile efficiency. Senator Gray was sequestered in the medical bay, being treated for the effects of the neurotoxin. Anne Austin was resting, her arm elevated, while Elias Vance worked feverishly in the command center.

Charlotte Reed stood before the large digital map Elias used to track the intelligence movements. The screen displayed four key elements:

1. Townhome 21: Red circle, confirmed operative base.
2. Lomax Jr.: Blinking red dot, confirmed operative location (last seen near the Federal Annex).
3. Fitzgerald: New red dot, active satellite tracker detected in a D.C. parking structure (a signal from his abandoned SUV).
4. The D.O.J. Target: A glowing green circle, representing the office of Deputy Director Samuel Thorne (no relation to the previous fictional character), the high-ranking D.O.J. official Judge Vance had compelled to initiate the national security inquiry.

Elias looked up from his console, holding the fragile, tiny mirror drive. "The full decryption is complete, Charlotte. We have it all. The *Perseus Protocol* memo, the $500,000 coercion proof, the schematics for the staged murder, and the liquidation codes Wilfred stole. The proof of Judge Lomax's treason is irrefutable."

"Good," Charlotte said, her voice strained. She had not slept, but the urgency of the moment had burned away her fatigue. "Now, the hard part. We have to make Senator Gray talk. We have to find the ledger."

She walked into the medical bay where Senator Gray was sitting, looking small and defeated, the presidential sheen entirely gone.

"Senator," Charlotte began, pulling a chair close. "We have proof that James Fitzgerald tried to assassinate you this morning using a neurotoxin. Fitzgerald is the Gatekeeper, the man who handed the key to the killer, Lomax Jr. Your aide, the man you trusted for thirty years, was planning to eliminate you to protect the network."

Gray paled, gripping the sheets. "I—I can't believe it. Thirty years... why? What network?"

"The one that paid for your campaign, Senator," Charlotte said, maintaining a relentless focus. "The one that routed money through 21 Holdings LLC in Belgrade. You are an Asset, Senator. The murder of Sarah Jenkins was a cleanup operation, and the trial was a shield. We have the proof of the conspiracy, but we lost the final financial link—the ledger in your destroyed briefcase."

Charlotte leaned in, her eyes commanding. "Tell me about the money, Senator. Fitzgerald was a deep asset. He had to have a backup of that ledger. Where did he keep the only documents that prove you were a knowing, willing accomplice to a foreign power?"

Senator Gray began to weep, his chest heaving with deep, broken sobs. "I didn't know, Charlotte! I swear! I never knew about Belgrade! Fitzgerald managed everything. The money was routed through a series of shell committees—the Unity PAC, the Citizens for Governance PAC. He told me it was clean money from offshore venture capital."

"And the briefcase? Why was that ledger so important that Fitzgerald risked his life to throw it onto the roof? Why was Lomax Jr. there to destroy it?"

"Because that briefcase—that ledger—contained the real donor list," Gray whispered, the confession tearing out of him. "The list of every single politician, every committee chair, every lobbying firm that had received a cut of the Belgrade money over the last five years. It wasn't just my treason; it was the treason of the entire D.C. establishment. Fitzgerald called it the Covenant List."

Charlotte's breath caught. The Covenant List. Not a single financial ledger, but a web of political corruption so vast it could shatter the Senate and the Intelligence Committees—the very people Fitzgerald had leveraged to hunt Elias Vance.

"And where is the backup of the Covenant List, Senator?" Charlotte pressed, her urgency mounting.

Gray shook his head weakly. "Fitzgerald kept it secured. He had a private security box at the Presidential Library in Dallas. He told me he placed a copy there years ago, the only place he felt was safe from D.C. surveillance. If anything ever happened to him, the library was the release mechanism."

Charlotte stood up, already moving for the door. A Presidential Library. A public, secured facility that would be untouchable by the *Perseus* network unless Fitzgerald personally retrieved it.

She looked at Anne, who was listening intently from the doorway. "Fitzgerald is heading for Egress now. He knows the mirror drive is safe. His next move is to retrieve the Covenant

List from Dallas before we do, and use it as his ultimate leverage against the entire U.S. government. We have to intercept him."

15:00—Elias Vance's Command Center, Virginia

Charlotte and Elias stood over the digital map. The red dot representing Fitzgerald's abandoned SUV was now static.

"He's using a burner vehicle," Elias confirmed, typing rapidly. "He's likely heading to Dulles Airport or a private airstrip. He needs to get to Dallas immediately."

"We need to stop him, but we can't use official channels," Charlotte said, pacing. "Fitzgerald has contacts inside the Senate Intelligence Committee; if we raise the alarm, he'll have the airport shut down, and the Covenant List destroyed before we get there."

"We have to use the evidence we have," Anne interjected, her voice firm. "The mirror drive. It's the only clean piece of evidence that can bypass the political layers and compel the D.O.J. to act immediately. We hand the mirror drive to Deputy Director Thorne, personally. We give them the Judge's treason, and we demand immediate federal jurisdiction over Fitzgerald and the retrieval of the Dallas List."

Charlotte nodded. "It's the only way to stop Fitzgerald legally. We trade the Judge's life for the network's exposure."

She looked at Elias. "Contact Deputy Director Thorne. Use the code word Judge Vance provided: *21st Amendment*. Tell him we have highly classified evidence of coercion and treason that must be reviewed personally, at a secure, neutral location, now."

The D.O.J. Hand-off (Charlotte Reed & Deputy Director Thorne)

17:00—The FBI's Secured Legal Annex, Quantico, Virginia

The rendezvous with Deputy Director Samuel Thorne was a tense, silent affair. Thorne was a career counter-intelligence officer, lean, gray, and radiating the weary professionalism of a man who had seen too much political corruption. He met Charlotte and Elias in a small, windowless interrogation room, flanked by two armed, silent agents.

Charlotte sat opposite him, placing the titanium container holding the mirror drive on the table.

"Deputy Director Thorne, I am Charlotte Reed, counsel for Senator Marcus David Gray. This drive contains the life and career of Federal Judge Joseph Lomax, Sr. More importantly, it contains the definitive proof of a foreign intelligence operation—Perseus—that coerced a sitting federal judge to control a murder trial and conceal a deep-state political insertion."

Thorne nodded curtly. "I am aware of the allegations from Judge Vance's order. They are extraordinary, Ms. Reed. You are accusing the judiciary of treason. You realize the gravity of these accusations?"

"I realize that the murder of Sarah Jenkins was a staged assassination to protect the network's Asset, Senator Gray, and that the killer is the Judge's son, Joseph Lomax Jr., whose crimes the Judge covered up years ago. The terminal data on this drive proves the coercion, the staging, and the entire Perseus structure."

She slid the drive across the table. "We offer you this evidence on two conditions. First, immediate, full immunity from the murder charge for Joseph Lomax Jr., in exchange for his full cooperation in exposing the entire network. Second, the immediate seizure of all assets and travel documents belonging to James Fitzgerald, Senator Gray's personal aide, who is the Gatekeeper of the network and is currently attempting Egress from D.C."

Thorne picked up the drive, examining the seals. "Why the urgency on Fitzgerald?"

"Because Fitzgerald has an unexposed, backup ledger—the Covenant List—containing the names of dozens of compromised U.S. political figures who have benefited from the Belgrade money. He keeps it in a secure location at the Presidential Library in Dallas. If he gets to Dallas, he destroys the list, and the entire network walks free."

Thorne looked at the drive, then back at Charlotte. "Ms. Reed, you have provided us with the ultimate leverage, but you are also confessing to massive obstruction of justice and suborning evidence by withholding this from the court for forty-eight hours."

"I withheld it from a compromised court, sir. Judge Lomax was the 21st Juror. My actions were necessary to ensure the evidence was not destroyed by the network," Charlotte countered, unflinching. "You want the treason charges against a U.S. Federal Judge? They are on that drive. You want the identity of the operative and the entire Belgrade network? It's all there. The clock is ticking on Fitzgerald. Do you take the deal?"

Thorne met her gaze. He had no choice. The integrity of the state was paramount. "The deal is accepted, Ms. Reed. We will initiate immediate Black Flag asset seizure against Fitzgerald and alert our Dallas field office to intercept the Covenant List. You and Mr. Vance are required to remain available to the Bureau. You are witnesses, but you are not yet cleared."

Charlotte felt the first, massive wave of relief wash over her. The legal battle was over. The intelligence war had begun.

The Convergence (Joseph Lomax Jr.)

18:30—Reagan National Airport, D.C.

Joseph Lomax Jr. was running on pure survival instinct. He had failed to retrieve the *J.L. Senior* terminal, his father had betrayed him, and now, his only remaining goal was to secure the stolen liquidation codes that Wilfred Sinclair possessed, and eliminate the new threat: James Fitzgerald.

He had received the emergency order from Fitzgerald (*Eliminate Asset Gray*) but had ignored it. Fitzgerald was no longer his superior; he was a potential rival for control of the network's remaining assets. Lomax Jr. had found Fitzgerald's secondary egress plan: a commercial flight scheduled to leave Reagan National for Dallas. Fitzgerald was retrieving the Covenant List.

Lomax Jr. located Fitzgerald in the crowded ticketing area, wearing the dark hoodie, blending seamlessly into the rush-hour travelers. Fitzgerald was holding a small, nondescript carry-on bag—the bag that likely held the encryption codes to the Covenant List, or perhaps the final, lethal neurotoxin.

Lomax Jr. moved with the cold, practiced ease of an assassin. He slipped into the crowd, closing the distance, his hand inside his coat, securing the silenced pistol. He planned a quick, silent injection—a heart attack—before Fitzgerald even reached the security line.

Just as Lomax Jr. reached Fitzgerald, a sudden, piercing alarm blared over the airport's public address system.

"Attention, all passengers! Security alert! James Fitzgerald, ticketed for Flight 322 to Dallas, is to report immediately to the D.O.J. Counter-Intelligence agents at Gate 45. All immediate surrounding areas are now under Black Flag lockdown! Repeat: James Fitzgerald is a Federal Material Witness under emergency seizure!"

The sound of sirens was immediate, echoing through the terminal. D.O.J. agents in full tactical gear—Thorne's team— swarmed the concourse, running toward Fitzgerald's location.

Fitzgerald's eyes darted frantically, realizing the D.O.J. had moved with unprecedented speed. Charlotte Reed had won. The seizure of the terminal had given them the speed, and the mention of the Covenant List had given them the political urgency.

He saw Lomax Jr. standing beside him, the look of murderous betrayal clear on the operative's face.

"You failed, Joey," Fitzgerald hissed, dropping his carry-on bag. "You lost the terminal, and now you've lost the Bench."

"You exposed us, Fitzgerald," Lomax Jr. countered, his hand closing around the pistol grip. "You are the Gatekeeper. You don't get to defect."

The D.O.J. agents were closing in, yelling commands.

Fitzgerald made his final move. He shoved Lomax Jr. hard into a nearby structural pillar, creating a chaotic diversion. He then ran toward the nearest emergency exit, drawing a small, explosive flashbang grenade from his hoodie pocket.

Lomax Jr. recovered instantly, raising his pistol, but the D.O.J. agents were now firing warning shots. He was pinned between the federal agents and his target.

Fitzgerald threw the flashbang grenade, not at the agents, but at the glass doors of the emergency exit. The explosion was deafening, shattering the glass and filling the terminal with smoke and the ringing echoes of chaos.

He sprinted through the gap, disappearing into the complex web of airport service tunnels.

Lomax Jr., stunned by the explosion, realized he was trapped. He was standing alone in the clearing smoke, his pistol exposed, surrounded by D.O.J. agents who had just witnessed him trying to eliminate the very material witness they were trying to seize.

"Freeze! Drop the weapon!" the agents screamed, their rifles trained on the Judge's son.

Lomax Jr. knew the fight was over. He dropped the pistol. The fanaticism was gone, replaced by a cold, defeated acceptance. He was immediately tackled, handcuffed, and dragged away. The trigger man was in custody.

The D.O.J. had failed to seize the Gatekeeper, but they had captured the killer, and they had secured the mirror drive. The entire *Perseus* network was now exposed.

The Final Reckoning (Charlotte Reed)

19:30—Elias Vance's Command Center, Virginia

Charlotte and Anne watched the news footage of the chaos at Reagan National: the flashbang explosion, the shattered glass, and the image of a defeated Joseph Lomax Jr. being hauled away by D.O.J. agents.

"Lomax Jr. is in custody. Fitzgerald is on the run, but his asset seizure is active," Charlotte summarized, her voice shaking slightly from the relief and the finality of the move. "Judge Lomax, Sr. is now under federal investigation. The

Covenant List remains unsecured in Dallas, but the D.O.J. is on the way."

"We did it, Charlotte," Anne said, a slow, exhausted smile touching her lips. "We broke the Bench. We exposed the treason."

"We broke the law to save the law, Anne," Charlotte replied, looking at the titanium container that now held the fate of the presidency. "Now, the real work begins. We have the coercion proof, and we have the killer, who is now being offered immunity in exchange for his testimony. The murder trial is a national security tribunal. The arraignment is now officially a hearing on treason."

Charlotte knew her perfect record was stained forever by the illegal alliance and the blackmail of the Judge, but the stakes had demanded it.

"What about the money, Charlotte?" Anne asked. "Wilfred Sinclair is still on the run with the liquidation codes and the millions in Belgrade money."

"Wilfred is a thief, but he's not a killer. He's our clean-up crew," Charlotte said, pulling up the satellite tracker Elias had placed on the stolen funds. "He left me the tip-off about the Belgrade money, he ran with the funds, and he left the network exposed. His final act of self-preservation was the best defense Senator Gray ever had. We let the D.O.J. chase Fitzgerald and the Covenant List. I'll chase Wilfred and the money."

She looked at Anne. "Now, we wait for the D.O.J. to clear Senator Gray of the murder charge, and for Judge Vance to move the trial from the criminal court to the Senate Intelligence Committee. The 21st Juror is broken, and the truth is finally public."

CHAPTER 14

The Covenant List

19:45—FBI Secured Legal Annex, Quantico, Virginia

The room was cold, sterile, and silent, the kind of environment designed to intimidate even the most hardened criminal. But Joseph Lomax Jr., shackled to the steel table, did not look intimidated. He looked like a martyr who had just failed his holy mission.

Across from him sat Deputy Director Samuel Thorne of the D.O.J. Counter-Intelligence Division, and two silent, heavily armed federal agents. Thorne held the slim, titanium case containing the mirror drive—the proof of Lomax Jr.'s treason and his father's coercion—and the only piece of leverage that mattered.

"Mr. Lomax," Thorne began, his voice calm, professional, and devoid of judgment. "Your father, Judge Joseph Lomax, Sr, has filed his recusal and is fully cooperating with the Bureau. He has provided details regarding the Perseus network's coercion, the payment to Belgrade, and your role in the liquidation of Sarah Jenkins. We know you did not act alone, and we know your involvement was a function of blackmail, not personal malice."

Lomax Jr. stared back, his eyes fixed and cold—the eyes of a fanatic. "My father is weak. He traded his nation for his son. He has no authority over me."

"He is trying to save your life, Joseph," Thorne corrected him, tapping the drive. "I have been authorized to offer you full, immediate immunity from the murder of Sarah Jenkins. The evidence of coercion is strong, and we believe you were forced to carry out the Phase One Retrieval sequence. In exchange for this immunity, you will provide us with the structure of the Perseus network, the identity of the Belgrade handlers, and the location of the primary assets. Specifically, James Fitzgerald."

Lomax Jr. laughed, a harsh, humorless sound that scraped against the silence of the room. "Immunity? I don't want immunity for doing my duty. Fitzgerald is the Gatekeeper. He is protecting the network from compromised weakness—men like my father, who value sentiment over structure. You want the network? You will have to cut it out of the nation's throat."

Thorne leaned forward, pushing a manila folder across the table. Inside was the memo Charlotte Reed had retrieved from the Judge's terminal: the document detailing the payment of $500,000 to cover Lomax Jr.'s five-year-old fraud charges.

"We know why you were coerced, Joseph," Thorne said softly. "You owe the network nothing. They didn't save you; they bought you. They owned your father for five years through your crime. Break the silence, and you walk free, serving your country, not your handlers."

The memo was the breaking point. Not the murder, not the treason, but the raw, exposed truth of his shame—the fact that his life was built on his father's desperation and a half-million dollar debt.

Lomax Jr.'s fanatical composure finally fractured. His shoulders slumped. "The network is self-sustaining. It doesn't need Belgrade anymore; it needs the Covenant List."

"The list of compromised politicians," Thorne confirmed, his pulse quickening. "Fitzgerald is heading to Dallas now to retrieve it. Where is the backup, Joseph? Be precise."

"The list is segmented. Fitzgerald had multiple copies. The primary, hard copy is stored in a private security box he rented years ago. Box 399. He kept it at the George W. Bush Presidential Library," Lomax Jr. admitted, his voice a dull monotone of defeat. "He used the library's secure storage facility—the irony appealed to his sense of operational theater. He believed it was the one place the D.C. political surveillance wouldn't dare touch."

"Box 399," Thorne repeated, nodding to one of his agents. "And the access code?"

Lomax Jr. looked up, his eyes regaining a sliver of their cold ruthlessness. "I have nothing more to say to the traitor's men. The network is secured. You may have the location, but you don't have Fitzgerald. And without him, the Covenant List is encrypted with a key that will die the moment he is captured or killed."

Thorne stood up. He had the location, the box number, and confirmation of Fitzgerald's goal. The interrogation was over. He looked down at the defeated assassin.

"You've made your choice, Joseph. You're trading your freedom for silence. I hope your loyalty keeps you warm in federal prison."

20:15—Elias Vance's Secure Location, Virginia

Charlotte Reed was still in the command center, the glow of

the digital map reflecting in her tired eyes. She was coordinating with Elias, who was sifting through the limited data found in Fitzgerald's abandoned carry-on bag from Reagan National: a clean passport, four hundred dollars cash, and a highly complex, multi-layered digital access key, likely for the Dallas security box.

The encrypted line from Deputy Director Thorne buzzed. Charlotte picked up instantly.

"Reed. Lomax Jr. has confirmed the target: Box 399 at the Presidential Library in Dallas. Fitzgerald is heading there now. We are deploying two D.O.J. Counter-Intelligence teams from Houston and Dallas to establish a secure perimeter. Fitzgerald has a head start and the access codes. He will reach the box within the hour."

"And the Covenant List is encrypted?" Charlotte asked, her voice tight.

"It is. Lomax Jr. won't give us the master key. Fitzgerald will destroy the list before capture. This is a containment mission, Ms. Reed. We need to seize the box, secure Fitzgerald, and then worry about the decryption."

Charlotte looked at Elias, who was holding the access key Fitzgerald had left behind. "Thorne, you have the tactical advantage, but you don't have the methodology. Fitzgerald is a ghost; he's been planning this egress for years. He will have a dead-man switch or an explosive charge on that box. If your teams approach conventionally, the Covenant List—the names of every compromised political figure in D.C.—will be turned to ash."

"Then what do you suggest, Ms. Reed? You are not authorized for an operational deployment."

"I suggest I am the only person Fitzgerald has consistently underestimated, and I am the only one who can anticipate his desperation," Charlotte countered, already grabbing her coat. "My entire defense strategy was built on defeating the network he created. Send me to Dallas. I will accompany your team, and I will be the one who opens Box 399. Fitzgerald will not anticipate the lawyer, and that moment of surprise will be our only chance to contain him before he presses the kill-switch on the list."

Thorne hesitated. Sending a defense attorney into an active counter-intelligence seizure operation was insane, but Charlotte Reed had already secured the Judge's recusal and delivered the killer. He needed her unique insight into the compromised minds of the network.

"Confirmed, Ms. Reed," Thorne said finally. "We will arrange immediate, secured transit to Dallas Love Field. You are now a Consultant with Federal Material Witness Status. You follow my team's orders, or you are arrested the moment you land."

21:00—Dallas Love Field, Texas

Charlotte landed on a private tarmac, stepping directly from the jet into a black, unmarked sedan, flanked by two armed, silent D.O.J. agents. The urgency was palpable. The city was calm, oblivious to the high-stakes intelligence operation converging on one of its most revered public institutions.

She was handed a detailed tactical blueprint of the Presidential Library's security storage facility. The vault was below ground, accessed only by a dedicated elevator and a multi-factor biometric lock. Box 399 was a double-size security deposit, located in the furthest corner of the vault.

"Fitzgerald is on the ground," Agent Reyes, the team leader, informed her, pointing to a blinking tactical marker on the tablet. "He used a private charter and is currently moving toward the Library. We have a full perimeter established, but he is outside it. We need to be inside the vault before he is."

"We won't beat him to the door, Agent Reyes," Charlotte stated, studying the blueprint. "Fitzgerald is the Gatekeeper. He knows the Library's infrastructure better than your team. He'll use a blind spot to slip past your perimeter. The only way we win is by anticipating his move inside the vault."

She pointed to the location of Box 399. "Fitzgerald's security is in the box itself. He knows he might be followed. He'll have a pressure sensor or an optic trigger inside Box 399 that instantly detonates the contents if the wrong code is entered or if the box is seized by force."

"So, we can't breach it," Agent Reyes concluded grimly.

"We can't touch it," Charlotte agreed. "We have to wait for Fitzgerald to open it, expose the list, and then contain him in the exact moment of his final vulnerability."

21:30—The Vault (James Fitzgerald)

James Fitzgerald moved through the empty, silent halls of the Presidential Library. He was not wearing a hoodie; he was in a sharp, dark suit, carrying an official-looking briefcase—the perfect picture of a senior political operative conducting sensitive, late-hour business. He had bypassed the security perimeter with contemptuous ease, using a service ID badge and codes that had been valid for twenty years.

He reached the vault elevator and descended into the cold, concrete depths of the archives.

The vault was massive, housing decades of historical documents, photographs, and artifacts. The security deposit boxes lined the back wall, glinting under the pale fluorescent light.

Fitzgerald walked directly to Box 399. He pulled out the custom biometric access key from his briefcase—the key Elias Vance had already studied—and placed his thumb on the scanner.

Access Granted. The box clicked open.

Fitzgerald did not hesitate. He had been planning this moment for years: the final act of control. Inside the box was not a financial ledger, but a slim, military-grade flash drive, encased in a pressure-sensitive resin—the Covenant List.

He pulled the drive out, his heart beating with triumphant certainty. With this list, he didn't just expose the Perseus network; he controlled it. He controlled the entire compromised political structure of the United States. He was no longer a gatekeeper; he was the Kingmaker.

He turned, the drive clutched in his hand, ready to leave.

"It's over, Fitzgerald."

Charlotte Reed stood ten feet away, flanked by Agent Reyes and two armed D.O.J. tactical agents. They had used the service tunnels in the blueprint to enter the vault moments before Fitzgerald arrived, sealing the exit.

Fitzgerald's composure cracked, his eyes widening in a rare moment of genuine, professional shock. "Reed? How did you... you're a lawyer. You should be in D.C. with your puppet client."

"Your puppet client, Senator Gray, is safe in Virginia, and your killer, Joseph Lomax Jr., is in federal custody," Charlotte stated, her voice echoing in the vast, silent vault. She held up her hands, palms open. "I'm here because I anticipated your final move. You lost, Fitzgerald. The Judge recused, the evidence is mirrored, and your treason is exposed. Drop the drive and surrender."

Fitzgerald, recovering instantly, saw the trap. He smiled, a cold, predatory grimace.

"You won the legal battle, Charlotte, but you don't understand the war. This drive, the Covenant List, is the nuclear option. It contains the names of six sitting Senators, ten Congressmen, and the head of the Senate Intelligence Committee, all on the Belgrade payroll. If I am captured, this drive is instantly decrypted, and the list is released to the public. If I am killed, the list is released. Your precious country collapses into a constitutional crisis before dawn."

He lifted the drive, holding it with two fingers over a small, custom-made device he had concealed in his suit cuff—a low-frequency electromagnetic pulse emitter.

"I have the final authority, Ms. Reed. If your team moves, this drive is wiped, and the public release sequence is activated. The choice is yours: save your career, or save the United States from implosion."

Agent Reyes raised his weapon, his finger tightening on the trigger. "Drop it now, Fitzgerald! That's an Order!"

"No, Agent Reyes!" Charlotte commanded, stepping forward, placing herself dangerously between the Agent and Fitzgerald. "He's telling the truth. The list must be secured intact."

She focused solely on Fitzgerald, using the same ruthless psychological warfare she had used on the Judge. "You're not a kingmaker, Fitzgerald. You're a frightened man running from a thirty-year debt. Wilfred Sinclair proved you were disposable. You were a Gatekeeper, not the architect. You think the network will allow you to run free with the Covenant List? They will track you, kill you, and pin the entire treason on your dead body."

"I am the network now!" Fitzgerald screamed, momentarily losing his composure.

Charlotte pressed the advantage. "Then prove it. Give the list to the D.O.J. and walk away. You're not a killer, Fitzgerald; you're an intelligence asset. Don't ruin your life's work with a flashbang and a flash drive. Surrender the list, and we secure your cooperation in bringing down the real handlers in Belgrade."

Fitzgerald hesitated, his eyes darting frantically from the drive to Charlotte's unblinking determination. He knew his capture was imminent, and his final revenge was too costly. He realized the terrifying paradox: the only way to save the network he had built was to cooperate with the authorities who were trying to destroy it.

He dropped his arm, his shoulders slumping in defeat.

"The Covenant List is yours, Ms. Reed," Fitzgerald whispered, placing the drive gently on the ground. "But the network is smarter than you know. You may have the list, but you don't have the money. Wilfred Sinclair is the final weakness. He has the liquidation codes, and he has the millions. Find the money, or the network will rebuild in a week."

Agent Reyes moved instantly, tackling Fitzgerald and securing the Covenant List drive in a titanium case. The Gatekeeper was secured.

23:00—FBI Secured Legal Annex, Dallas

Charlotte was on the plane back to D.C. She had the final piece of the puzzle: the Covenant List, safely in the D.O.J.'s hands, poised to expose the largest political scandal in a generation.

She had spoken briefly to Thorne before boarding. Joseph

Lomax Jr. was holding fast to his silence, but the D.O.J. had enough evidence to proceed. The murder charge against Senator Gray would be dropped, the focus shifting to the vast web of treason.

She sat in the private cabin, staring out at the dark, distant lights of the capital. The murder case was solved, the political conspiracy exposed, and her client, Senator Gray, was safe—innocent of murder, guilty of being an unknowing pawn.

But Fitzgerald's final warning echoed in her mind: *Wilfred Sinclair is the final weakness.*

Charlotte pulled out her personal secure phone and opened the tracker app Elias Vance had installed. It was a faint, intermittent signal, tracing the stolen Belgrade money. The signal had moved across the Atlantic, resting in a new, undisclosed location.

The single red dot on the map was now pulsing softly from a remote, sun-drenched coastal town. The financial architect was waiting.

Charlotte typed a single, final text message to Elias Vance.

Target: Monaco. Phase Two: Retrieval.

The legal war was over. The hunt for the money—the final, personal battle to reclaim her partner and the millions he had stolen—had just begun.

CHAPTER 15

The Monte Carlo Gamble (Charlotte Reed & Elias Vance)

23:45—FBI Secured Legal Annex, Quantico, Virginia

The adrenaline of the Dallas confrontation had subsided, leaving Charlotte Reed operating on the fumes of exhaustion and a deep, consuming sense of purpose. She sat opposite Deputy Director Samuel Thorne in a secure debriefing room, the titanium case containing the Covenant List resting between them—the definitive proof that half of D.C. political infrastructure was compromised by the Belgrade network.

"We have the Covenant List, Ms. Reed," Thorne stated, his voice tight with controlled disbelief. "The treason is now quantifiable. Fitzgerald is talking, albeit in cryptic terms, and Joseph Lomax Jr. is facing murder and espionage charges. You delivered the single largest domestic intelligence coup in a decade. Senator Gray will be cleared of the murder charge and quietly neutralized as a political factor. The work in Washington is finished."

Charlotte nodded, accepting the summation with a cold focus that Thorne found disconcerting. She didn't look like a victorious lawyer; she looked like a general planning the next offensive.

"The work in Washington is *contained*, Director Thorne. It is not finished," Charlotte countered, leaning forward. "Fitzgerald's final warning was the most critical piece of intelligence we retrieved. The Perseus network is not primarily political; it is financial. They don't need Gray anymore, but they absolutely need the money that sustains their operations. Wilfred Sinclair stole over twenty million dollars of their liquidation funds and holds the master encryption codes for the entire Belgrade ledger."

Elias Vance, seated beside Charlotte, confirmed the analysis. "Wilfred used a sophisticated, peer-to-peer crypto-liquidation sequence. It wasn't a panicked withdrawal; it was a planned, professional theft of the network's emergency exit capital. He ran because he was next on Lomax Jr.'s hit list, but he also ran with their keys. If that money is not recovered, and if those codes are not secured, the network—even without the Covenant List—will rebuild within three months using untraceable digital infrastructure. They'll just install a new Asset."

Thorne looked grim. "Sinclair is a fugitive, Ms. Reed. He is an associate in a major federal investigation, and we have international warrants out for his arrest on charges of larceny and grand financial fraud. Where is he?"

Charlotte pulled up the satellite tracker Elias had installed on the Belgrade funds—a device designed to trail the conversion of the stolen cryptocurrency into hard asset transfers. The map displayed a single, pulsing red dot over the French Riviera.

"He is in Monaco, Director Thorne," Charlotte stated. "The destination is not a coincidence. Monaco has some of the most aggressive financial secrecy laws in the world. He has placed himself in a jurisdiction where U.S. federal warrants are often dismissed as political nuisances. He is not just hiding; he is laundering the money, making it untouchable, and waiting for the dust to settle."

"Monaco is beyond my immediate jurisdiction," Thorne admitted, running a weary hand over his face. "We can initiate contact with Interpol and the Monegasque authorities, but the process will be slow. Sinclair will be untouchable within a week."

"Exactly," Charlotte pressed. "The legal approach is too slow. The political exposure of the Covenant List will cripple the network, but only the recovery of the money will starve it. I am no longer operating as Senator Gray's counsel, Director. I am operating as the only person who understands Wilfred's methodology and mindset. I am the only one he might not immediately eliminate."

She made her final demand. "I need a window, Director. I need a secured, classified agreement that allows me to pursue Wilfred Sinclair to Monaco, retrieve the stolen funds and the master codes, and deliver them to your office. In exchange, I demand a guarantee that any potential obstruction charges against me or Detective Austin, related to our extra-legal acquisition of the mirror drive and the coercion of Judge Lomax, will be permanently shelved."

Thorne stared at her. The lawyer who had just broken the judicial branch was now demanding federal immunity for her crimes in exchange for finishing the intelligence job. He smiled faintly, a slow, grudging acknowledgment of her ruthless pragmatism.

"You're asking for a diplomatic nightmare, Ms. Reed," Thorne said. "But you are also the only key left. Consider the deal accepted. Elias Vance is now officially detached from this investigation, and you are acting as an unsupervised *Consultant on Foreign Asset Retrieval.*"

Charlotte stood, sealing the agreement with a single, sharp nod. The legal chapter was closed. The hunt was on.

04:00—Elias Vance's Secured Hangar, Northern Virginia

Charlotte was standing beside a sleek, unmarked Gulfstream jet, watching Elias Vance pack two anonymous duffel bags with equipment. Anne Austin, her arm now set in a professional cast, stood nearby, insisting on helping with the final logistical checks.

"I hate that I'm not coming," Anne admitted, the frustration evident in her voice. "Fitzgerald warned you—Wilfred is the final weakness. He knows he's the target of both sides. He'll be armed, and he'll be paranoid."

"You are the ultimate weakness, Anne," Charlotte corrected her, placing a hand gently on Anne's cast. "You are the only person who can brief Thorne, ensure the Judge's son faces justice, and protect Senator Gray from the inevitable backlash. Your fight is here. Mine is personal."

Elias zipped up the last bag, placing it in the jet's cargo hold. "Wilfred isn't a soldier, Charlotte. He's a financial architect. His defense mechanism is complexity, not confrontation. He won't be hiding in a bunker; he'll be hiding behind a dozen shell corporations and a jurisdiction that shields him."

Elias pulled up the latest financial data on his tablet—a complex flow chart showing the twenty million dollars being routed through three distinct Monegasque banks. "He moved the money fast, but he left a signature. He moved the money into a series of bearer bond accounts—untraceable assets that require physical presentation of a certificate for withdrawal. He's not waiting for a bank transfer. He's waiting for the physical paperwork to be finalized."

"So, he can't access the money until the certificates are

generated and delivered," Charlotte concluded. "That gives us a clock."

"Exactly. And the final delivery point for the certificates is a private vault in Monte Carlo. The delivery is scheduled for seventy-two hours from now," Elias confirmed. "We have three days to intercept him."

Charlotte boarded the Gulfstream, the interior luxurious but functional. She took a seat and pulled out the crumpled note Wilfred had left her days ago: *Don't trust the Bench.* His final act was to point her to the corruption he was fleeing. Now, she was pursuing the man who had been her partner for fifteen years—a man who had traded his career, his firm, and his loyalty for a suitcase full of stolen money.

"Monaco is less about wealth and more about discretion, Elias," Charlotte said, watching the hangar disappear beneath them as the jet lifted off. "Wilfred thinks he's invisible there. We're going to prove him wrong."

06:00 (Local Time) – Somewhere Over the Atlantic

The flight was quiet, long, and provided Charlotte with the first genuine rest she'd had in a week. Yet, sleep was fitful, disturbed by the ghost of Wilfred's calculated betrayal.

She pulled out her personal file on Wilfred, searching for any vulnerability that wasn't financial. He had always been impeccably structured, devoid of the vices that destroyed other powerful men. He had no family, no hobbies beyond vintage watches, and no emotional entanglements.

"Wilfred's genius was always his anonymity," Charlotte observed, sharing the file with Elias. "He was the perfect ghost in a high-profile firm. How did he know Sarah Jenkins was the one to pay off the Belgrade money? Why was he the one chosen to steal the liquidation codes?"

Elias, who had been analyzing the Belgrade bank transfers, looked up. "He wasn't chosen, Charlotte. He *was* the financial architect of the Perseus network inside the U.S. He created 21 Holdings LLC. Sarah Jenkins was his subordinate—his treasurer, not the asset manager. When the network liquidated Sarah, Wilfred knew the ledger was exposed, and he was next. So, he stole the funds he himself had managed for years."

"The perfect crime," Charlotte murmured. "Rob the very network you helped build, using the system you created."

"And he used his final act to save you," Elias added. "The tip about Belgrade, the note about the Judge—it was self-preservation, yes, but also a professional courtesy. He ensured his own network was too busy chasing treason to hunt him down before he reached Monaco."

10:30 (Local Time) – Nice Côte d'Azur Airport, France

The Gulfstream landed seamlessly in Nice, the nearest international hub to the Principality of Monaco. The air was warm, smelling of salt and expensive perfume—a stark contrast to the gritty desperation of Washington.

Charlotte and Elias passed through customs with discreet speed, using the cover provided by Deputy Director Thorne—official diplomatic passports granting them immediate access for "sensitive consulting."

They secured an unmarked sedan and made the thirty-minute drive along the winding, dizzyingly beautiful coastal roads into Monaco. The Principality was a high-gloss jewel box of marinas, opulent casinos, and towering residential glass. Every street, every building, was a testament to extreme wealth and extreme discretion.

"Welcome to the land of no questions asked," Elias commented, navigating the tight, crowded streets of Monte

Carlo. "Wilfred will assume his financial walls are impenetrable here. No one cares about a D.C. political murder. They care about their capital gains."

Elias set up their forward operating base in a discreetly rented apartment overlooking the Port Hercule—the massive marina filled with superyachts. He immediately launched a deep-scan analysis, focusing not on digital communications (which Wilfred would have secured), but on transactional anomalies within the banking sector.

"Wilfred has to pay for his safe haven," Elias explained, setting up a series of satellite dishes on the terrace. "He is using a limited credit card tied to a Monegasque shell corporation. He will need a secure residence and high-end services. I'll track the pattern of his spending to pinpoint his physical location."

The city's security systems were immense—every street corner, every lobby, every ATM was covered by sophisticated cameras. This was a city designed to catch petty thieves and protect multi-millionaires.

Within an hour, Elias had triangulated the spending. "Got him. He's booked into a hyper-luxury penthouse at the Tour Odéon—the tallest, most expensive residential tower in the city. Penthouse 48. Renting for seventy-five thousand a month. The anonymity is absolute, the security is brutal, and the view is spectacular."

"Penthouse 48," Charlotte repeated, looking up at the imposing, twin-towered glass monolith dominating the skyline. "He's hiding in plain sight. He's making a statement."

15:00—Tour Odéon Perimeter

Charlotte and Elias sat in the sedan, observing the entrance of the Tour Odéon. The entrance was guarded by three layers of private security, biometric access, and a bulletproof, revolving door. Getting inside would be impossible without a direct confrontation.

"We need a way in, Elias," Charlotte said. "We can't approach him conventionally. He'll see us coming, destroy the codes, and vanish back into the financial ether."

Elias pulled up the building's security schematics on his tablet, his eyes narrowed in concentration. "The building is sealed, but there's one vulnerability: the private maintenance lift that runs to the penthouse cleaning service. It requires a specific, temporary access key for a scheduled service call."

Just as Elias began running a bypass sequence on the building's maintenance network, his monitor flashed a rapid, alarming warning: HIGH-FREQUENCY SATELLITE PING DETECTED. BELGRADE ORIGIN. LOCATION TRIANGULATION: 500M AND CLOSING.

"We've been found," Elias hissed, slamming the laptop shut. "It's a Perseus network tracker. They aren't just monitoring the funds; they're monitoring the airspace around the funds. They know Wilfred is here, and they know the codes are in Monaco."

Charlotte looked out the window. A matte-black sedan, the same model as the one Fitzgerald had used in D.C., was pulling slowly up the avenue, its polarized windows concealing the occupants.

"Wilfred is not the only one hunting the liquidation codes," Charlotte realized. "Fitzgerald's failure and Lomax Jr.'s capture must have initiated an emergency response. They've sent a clean-up crew from Belgrade."

"They're here for the same reason we are," Elias confirmed, his voice urgent. "To eliminate Wilfred and secure the funds. We are now in a three-way race for Penthouse 48."

Charlotte stared at the black sedan, the cold dread of renewed personal danger settling over her. She pulled a silk scarf from her handbag, wrapping it tightly around her neck, using the habitual gesture to restore her focus.

"The Belgrade crew is operating on speed, Elias. They will go hard, fast, and violent. They won't care about Monegasque law. That gives us a unique advantage: we have to be the second team in. We let the Belgrade crew force their way into the penthouse, and we use the resulting chaos to secure Wilfred and the codes."

"That's suicide, Charlotte. You'll be walking into a gunfight."

"No," Charlotte said, meeting his gaze with a lethal resolve. "I'll be walking into a distraction. Wilfred won't be expecting me to walk into the middle of an assassination attempt. It's the only way to surprise him."

She pointed to the black sedan now pausing at the intersection, their eyes scanning the Tour Odéon.

"We let them breach the building. You focus on securing the maintenance lift key. I'm going in to face my partner. This is no longer a search for the truth; it's a fight for the money that sustains the treason."

The countdown had begun. The beautiful, opulent facade of Monaco was about to shatter, revealing the desperate, deadly intelligence war raging beneath its surface. The final confrontation was only hours away.

CHAPTER 16

The Architect's Lure (Charlotte Reed & Wilfred Sinclair)

16:00—Tour Odéon Perimeter, Monte Carlo

The sun, dropping towards the Mediterranean horizon, cast a blinding, high-gloss reflection off the massive, curved glass façade of the Tour Odéon. The residential tower, the tallest and most exclusive in Monaco, was an inverted monument to the world's quiet money, a place where fortunes were not made but silently preserved.

Charlotte Reed, seated low in the unmarked sedan, watched the matte-black saloon car—the one Elias Vance had identified as belonging to the Belgrade Retrieval Unit—pull into a private parking area two hundred meters from the Tour Odéon entrance. Four men emerged. They were not tourists, nor were they diplomats. They were professionals: large, silent, and wearing expensive, anonymous suits that failed to conceal the hard, disciplined movement of trained security operators. They carried briefcases, but the cold precision of their entry movements suggested the contents were not financial ledgers.

"That's the advance team, Charlotte," Elias murmured, his eyes fixed on the infrared satellite feed displayed on the tactical tablet. "The main asset transfer is still seventy-two hours out, but the network got nervous after Fitzgerald's failure. They're here to eliminate Wilfred Sinclair, secure the liquidation codes, and initiate an immediate, remote transfer of the stolen twenty million before the D.O.J. can compel the Monegasque banks to freeze the assets."

"Wilfred knew they would track the money," Charlotte said, watching the operatives disappear into the shadowed service entrance of a neighboring boutique hotel. She pulled the silk scarf tighter around her neck, a nervous, professional habit. "He placed the money into bearer bonds, ensuring physical certificates had to be presented for withdrawal. He's forced them to come here, to Monte Carlo. This isn't hiding; it's a brilliant, highly expensive lure."

Elias confirmed her analysis, his fingers flying across a custom-built signal jamming device. "He's hiding in the most visible, secured location in the Principality—Penthouse 48 of the Tour Odéon. The building has three levels of biometric security. The primary security detail is armed, professional, and loyal only to the building's owners. The Belgrade crew will have to breach every layer, creating the perfect window of distraction for us."

The high-stakes game had shifted again. Charlotte was no longer the defense attorney; she was an operative in an intelligence war, forced to rely on the chaotic violence of her enemies to save the life of the very man who had stolen millions and abandoned her.

"We let them breach, Elias. We let them create the noise," Charlotte decided, her voice firm. "You focus on the only vulnerability: the private maintenance lift. It runs from the sub-level service tunnel directly to the penthouse floor. It's too discreet for the building's main security desk to monitor continuously, and the Belgrade team won't use it; they'll go loud and fast, assuming Wilfred is the only threat."

Elias nodded, his expression grim. "I'm running a low-frequency signal emulator now. I can mimic the maintenance key's pulse, but I can only hold the lift for sixty seconds on the penthouse floor before the system initiates a full lockdown. That's your window, Charlotte. Sixty seconds to neutralize the Belgrade crew, secure Wilfred, and retrieve the codes."

Charlotte looked at the towering glass monolith of the Tour Odéon, where her former partner sat waiting, the ultimate prize in a desperate game. "If I walk into that penthouse during an assassination attempt, Wilfred will assume I'm part of the clean-up crew. I have to make him believe I'm there to save him. The only way to do that is to give him the one thing he didn't factor into his brilliant plan."

She thought of the conversation with Judge Lomax, Sr, and the confession of James Fitzgerald being the Gatekeeper. She needed one final, devastating truth that would shatter Wilfred's composure and force his cooperation.

19:00—The Penthouse Pre-Op (Wilfred Sinclair)

Inside Penthouse 48, Wilfred Sinclair looked down upon the glittering, artificial majesty of Monte Carlo. The apartment was vast, minimalist, and silent, the kind of place designed to make one feel omnipotent. He sat not on the expansive white sofa, but at a discreet, industrial-grade metal table set up in the secured, windowless utility room.

Before him lay his final project: the Belgrade Liquidation Codes. A single, small, highly secure flash drive, containing the key to the twenty million dollars and the encrypted master ledger of the entire Perseus financial infrastructure.

He had been watching the traffic below through a thermal scanner. He saw the matte-black saloon car. He saw the four professional operators. He knew the network had found him. He had planned for this.

Wilfred was not a killer, but he was a survivor, and his survival was engineered. He had given Charlotte Reed the tip about the Belgrade money, he had fled with the funds, and he had maneuvered the final asset transfer to Monaco, precisely to draw the network into an exposed confrontation. He was waiting not for the D.O.J., but for the final architect of the Perseus network—the person he knew would arrive to personally retrieve the stolen funds.

He pulled up the financial flow chart he had created years ago, detailing the initial $30 million seed money that funded 21 Holdings LLC. He had been loyal to the mission for nearly two decades, building the financial fortress that funded the political insertion. But when the network killed Sarah Jenkins, the woman he had recruited and silently cared for, he knew they had breached their own ethical code. His act of theft was an act of revenge, a way to lure the ultimate, protected target into the open.

He smiled, a thin, cold expression. The assassination attempt was now a highly controlled environment.

He checked the internal defenses: the motion sensors were off, the internal alarm was isolated, and he had planted a dozen explosive, non-lethal flashbang charges in the entrance corridor, designed to disorient and slow the incoming team.

Wilfred reached into his suit pocket, pulling out a sealed, official-looking document. It wasn't a bank statement. It was a Waiver of Extradition Immunity signed by a small, European nation's judicial representative—a document guaranteeing safe passage and immunity for one specific individual, in exchange for irrefutable evidence of transnational crimes.

Wilfred was not planning on retirement. He was planning on defection. He intended to deliver the entire financial network to an international court in exchange for his own freedom. And he needed a powerful, undeniable witness to his handover—someone the D.O.J. would trust.

He needed Charlotte Reed.

The primary access door to the penthouse suite, a heavy, soundproofed composite, suddenly shuddered. A faint, high-pitched mechanical whine followed, indicating a powerful hydraulic breach tool had been engaged.

The attack had begun.

Wilfred placed the liquidation codes and the signed waiver into a small, interior pocket of his jacket. He grabbed a pair of custom-built, noise-dampening earplugs and slipped them into his ears.

He walked to the utility room doorway, positioned perfectly behind the steel service counter, waiting for the blast. He could hear the distinct sound of tactical boots moving rapidly in the hallway outside.

The final phase of the Perseus Protocol was now activated.

19:05—The Breach and the Ascent (Elias Vance & Charlotte Reed)

Elias Vance sat in the service tunnel below the Tour Odéon, his fingers working furiously on the custom signal emulator. The low-frequency jamming pulse was active, masking his presence from the building's central security AI.

A massive, echoing *BOOM* resonated through the tunnel's concrete structure—the sound of the Belgrade crew breaching the penthouse door.

"They're in, Charlotte! Go!" Elias commanded, watching

the digital indicator jump from *SECURED* to *CHAOS* on the building schematics.

Charlotte, dressed in non-descript but highly durable black clothing, carrying only a small trauma kit and a powerful taser disguised as a cosmetic case, was already in the small maintenance lift. She had secured the temporary access key into the lift's system, overriding the standard security protocols.

The lift began its silent, terrifyingly fast ascent, shooting straight up the interior shaft of the Tour Odéon.

"The Belgrade crew is encountering resistance, Charlotte," Elias reported through her earpiece, his voice strained. "They hit a sequence of flashbangs. They're disoriented, but they're moving. They'll be on Wilfred in sixty seconds."

Charlotte's focus was absolute. She wasn't thinking about the gunfight above her; she was thinking about Wilfred's mind.

Why Monaco? Why bearer bonds?

Wilfred hadn't just exposed the network; he had exposed himself. He wanted the network to find him here. And he wanted Charlotte to arrive the moment they did.

"Elias, analyze the final transfer point for the bearer bonds," Charlotte ordered, her voice low and steady. "Why a private vault in Monte Carlo? Why not Zurich or Dubai?"

Elias typed rapidly. "Because the final, physical transfer of the certificates is scheduled to be overseen by a specific international financial lawyer known for extreme discretion— a woman named Dr. Katya Petrova. She's the only one who can legally compel the transfer of the funds."

Charlotte felt the sudden, shocking jolt of realization. "Dr. Katya Petrova. Wilfred wouldn't trust her with the final assets unless he knew her. Check the Belgrade financial flow chart, Elias. The one Wilfred gave me the tip about—the one Sarah

Jenkins made the $450,000 payment to."

Elias quickly cross-referenced the names. "The $450,000 payment to 21 Holdings LLC in Belgrade? The one with the untraceable crypto conversion?"

"Look at the transaction details before the crypto conversion. I need the original, untraced recipient of that money. Who was the ultimate beneficiary of the initial, seed funding?"

The ascent was agonizingly slow, the lift now passing the 40th floor. Above her, muffled sounds of a violent, close-quarters firefight were now audible through the soundproofed walls.

Elias's voice returned, laced with utter disbelief. "Charlotte. The initial, untraceable recipient account for the $450,000 payment, the person Sarah Jenkins was paying off... was a private shell corporation listed under the full legal name of Dr. Katya Petrova."

The lift slammed to a smooth, silent halt. Penthouse 48.

Charlotte didn't need to ask the rest of the question. Dr. Katya Petrova was not just the lawyer handling the final transfer. She was the financial core of the Perseus network—the true, ultimate architect of the Belgrade money flow. Wilfred hadn't lured a retrieval team; he had lured the Kingpin of the entire financial operation to Monaco.

Charlotte grabbed the taser, her heart pounding with a sudden, dangerous exhilaration. She wasn't here to save Wilfred. She was here to capture the true head of the network.

19:10—The Penthouse Showdown (Charlotte Reed & Wilfred Sinclair)

Charlotte slipped out of the maintenance lift and into a darkened service corridor adjacent to the penthouse utility room. The air here smelled acrid, thick with the sharp tang of burned sulfur from the flashbangs and the metallic scent of fresh gunpowder.

She moved quickly, silently, toward the light spilling from the utility room door. She could hear the rapid, controlled burst of automatic gunfire and the frantic screams of the Belgrade crew.

She peered around the corner. The massive, open-plan living room was a scene of utter chaos. The Belgrade crew—three men—were pinned down behind an expensive, shattered marble bar, firing suppressed weapons toward the utility room entrance.

In the center of the room, standing exposed and holding a sleek, silver, non-lethal gas disperser, was Wilfred Sinclair. He had the eyes of a desperate man who was finally, beautifully executing his final revenge.

Wilfred saw her instantly. His eyes widened, not in fear, but in pure, unadulterated shock. He had anticipated the Belgrade crew, but he had never factored in her presence.

"Charlotte! What the hell are you doing here?" Wilfred yelled, his voice strained against the gunfire.

Charlotte ignored the question, sprinting across the chaos toward the utility room, ducking low behind a crushed velvet ottoman. She pointed past Wilfred, toward the far, glass-walled conference room of the penthouse, which offered a secure, quiet alcove.

"Petrova is coming, Wilfred! Dr. Katya Petrova! The final beneficiary of the $450,000. She's the architect of the entire financial network, not Fitzgerald! You lured her here with the bearer bonds, didn't you?"

Wilfred's face, etched with fear and adrenaline, instantly transformed into a look of absolute, terrifying confirmation.

"She's the money, Charlotte! She's the one who killed Sarah! I lured her here for a clean surrender, and now her clean-up crew is trying to take the codes!"

He took a desperate step back, firing a large burst of concentrated, low-toxicity aerosol gas from his silver disperser directly at the pinned Belgrade crew. The gas was designed to cause instant, non-lethal disorientation and vomiting. The operatives dropped their weapons, choking and convulsing behind the marble bar.

The sudden silence was deafening, broken only by the sound of the men retching and Wilfred's labored breathing.

Charlotte rushed into the utility room, grabbing Wilfred by the shoulder, forcing him against the steel counter. "The codes, Wilfred! Give me the master liquidation codes and the full ledger!"

Wilfred pulled the small flash drive and the signed waiver from his jacket. "The money isn't for me, Charlotte! It's the network's lifeblood! I stole it to give her leverage! I set up this entire thing—the bearer bonds, the Monaco transfer, the whole damned operation—to force Petrova to come here, to meet me at the transfer desk so I could hand over the network to the international authorities and expose her! I needed a witness!"

He thrust the codes and the signed defection waiver into Charlotte's hand. "The waiver guarantees me immunity in exchange for the full financial ledger! I brought her here to betray her! You're my witness, Charlotte! You're the final piece of my defense!"

Charlotte looked down at the documents, her perfect defense record forgotten. Wilfred hadn't been an ordinary thief; he had been a double-agent, a financial architect who had engineered his own capture and his own revenge, using her as the reluctant executioner.

"Where is Petrova, Wilfred? Where is the real target?"

"She's in the building," Wilfred gasped, running a shaking hand over his face. "She was waiting for the clean-up report to confirm the codes were secured. She's on the move now! She's coming for the codes herself!"

Just as Wilfred finished the sentence, the service corridor door, which Charlotte had just entered through, was thrown violently open.

A woman stood in the doorway: tall, elegant, dressed in an immaculate, ice-blue suit, her features sharp, her eyes a cold, calculating gray. She carried a small, highly customized pistol with a gold inlay. It was Dr. Katya Petrova, the final architect of the Perseus network, the ultimate beneficiary of the millions, and the true Kingpin. She looked past the retching Belgrade crew, past the devastated living room, and focused entirely on the betrayal taking place in the utility room.

Petrova raised the gold-inlaid pistol, aiming directly at Wilfred's head.

"You pathetic fool, Wilfred," Petrova said, her voice a low, precise, Russian-inflected purr. "You thought I would risk twenty years of insertion for twenty million dollars? The money is the price of the mission. But you, my dear financial architect, are the traitor."

She fired a single, silenced shot.

Charlotte reacted instantly, throwing herself forward and knocking Wilfred to the floor. The bullet meant for Wilfred's head slammed into the steel counter where he had been standing, ricocheting harmlessly off the reinforced metal.

But Petrova was already moving, sprinting across the utility room toward the fallen figures. She was not aiming for them now; she was aiming for the one thing that mattered.

She was aiming for the liquidation codes that Charlotte now clutched in her hand.

The final battle for the financial lifeblood of the Perseus network had begun, and Charlotte Reed was trapped between the dying operatives, the fanatic architect, and the fate of her betrayed partner.

CHAPTER 17

The Final Architect (Charlotte Reed & Dr. Katya Petrova)

19:10—Tour Odéon Penthouse, Monte Carlo

The sound of the silenced pistol shot, followed by the metallic *thunk* of the ricochet off the steel counter, was terrifyingly close. Charlotte Reed lay sprawled across the floor of the utility room, the desperate momentum of her dive having saved Wilfred Sinclair's life—and almost certainly, her own.

Wilfred lay beneath her, coughing roughly, the shock of the near-fatal execution overriding the pain of the assault. The flash drive containing the Belgrade Liquidation Codes and his signed Waiver of Extradition Immunity was still clutched in Charlotte's hand.

Across the utility room, silhouetted against the ambient glow of the Monaco sunset, stood Dr. Katya Petrova. The architect of the Perseus network's financial structure was a vision of lethal elegance—ice-blue suit, sharp features, and the gold-inlaid pistol now aimed steadily at Charlotte's head.

Petrova did not rush. She stepped carefully over a trailing utility cord, her eyes fixed on the flash drive in Charlotte's hand. She was the ultimate professional: calm, precise, and utterly ruthless.

"The flash drive, Ms. Reed," Petrova commanded, her voice a low, hard purr, stripped of any diplomatic pretense. "Toss it to me, or I will ensure you spend the rest of your life answering for the criminal coercion of a sitting Federal Judge."

"You're too late, Doctor," Charlotte shot back, forcing herself into a kneeling position, pulling Wilfred slightly behind her. Her mind, fueled by sheer, desperate will, was already calculating the angles. "The coercion evidence is already mirrored and submitted to the D.O.J. The Judge recused. Your Gatekeeper, James Fitzgerald, is on the run, and your executioner, Joseph Lomax Jr., is in federal custody, singing for immunity. Your network is collapsing, and the only thing that matters now is the money, which I currently hold."

Petrova's composure fractured into a thin, predatory smile. "A lawyer's bluff. You are a defense counsel, Ms. Reed, not an intelligence operative. You cannot fathom the depth of the capital I control. The liquidation codes, the codes Wilfred so foolishly stole, are the master key to twenty million dollars of operating capital. Without them, the network stalls, yes. But without the money, *you* have no leverage. You want immunity for your detective friend and your career? You need that drive. Now, stand down."

"You're wrong," Charlotte said, looking quickly at the three Belgrade operatives writhing and choking near the shattered marble bar in the living room—disoriented but slowly recovering from Wilfred's gas. "I don't need the money. I need you. You're the Kingpin. Lomax Jr. and Fitzgerald are pawns. You're the final asset. I have the proof that you were the ultimate beneficiary of the $450,000 paid by the victim, Sarah Jenkins. That makes you the orchestrator of a state-sponsored murder. I will trade the liquidation codes for your surrender to Interpol."

Petrova laughed, a short, sharp sound of utter contempt.

She took one deliberate step closer, closing the gap to under ten feet.

"You are still playing by the rules of the D.C. courtroom, Ms. Reed. Here, there are no rules. Only survival."

She raised the pistol higher, aiming for Charlotte's shoulder—a non-fatal hit designed to force compliance.

Charlotte acted instinctively, using the only weapon she had left: the taser disguised as a cosmetic case. She had been holding it loosely in her left hand. She triggered the deployment, and two thin, electrified darts shot out, catching Petrova not in the torso, but in the thick, padded shoulder of the ice-blue suit.

The taser charge, designed for civilian use, was insufficient to stop a hardened operative, but the sudden, sharp shock caused Petrova to cry out and involuntarily jerk the trigger. The bullet slammed into the ceiling, showering the utility room in plaster dust and forcing Charlotte to pull Wilfred flat against the floor again.

The momentary confusion was enough. Charlotte scrambled backward, pulling Wilfred with her, retreating toward the darkened service corridor where the maintenance lift was located.

"Elias!" Charlotte screamed into her secured earpiece, the sound of the ricochet ringing in her ears. "Lift now! Penthouse floor! We're coming out!"

19:15—The Confession of the Thief

Wilfred, coughing violently, dragged himself against the wall, his eyes fixed on the raging figure of Petrova, who was slowly pulling the taser darts from her suit jacket, her face a mask of white-hot fury.

"She's coming, Charlotte," Wilfred gasped, clutching his side. "She's not a soldier; she's a sociopath. She won't stop until she has those codes. She built the entire financial system to make herself untouchable."

"Why, Wilfred? Why did you steal the money if you knew she would simply kill you for it?" Charlotte demanded, not looking away from the doorway. She had to understand the final betrayal.

Wilfred reached up, pulling his jacket open, revealing the empty internal pocket where the codes had been stored seconds ago. "It wasn't about the money, Charlotte. It was about Sarah Jenkins."

His voice dropped, thick with genuine, overwhelming grief. "Sarah was my recruit. I brought her into the firm, and I brought her into the network—telling her it was a long-term economic insertion strategy. When she realized the true depth of the foreign control, she panicked. She was trying to warn Gray—to defect, and use the $450,000 as her own leverage. Petrova knew she was compromised, and Petrova ordered Lomax Jr. to eliminate her."

"Petrova killed her because she was trying to defect," Charlotte concluded.

"Worse. Petrova killed her to send a message to me," Wilfred whispered, the full, devastating truth finally revealed. "Petrova wasn't just my co-conspirator; she was my controller. She recruited me twenty years ago when I was a struggling law student, deep in debt. She was the one who engineered the $500,000 cover-up for Lomax Jr.'s fraud, leveraging his father. She controlled the entire chess board. And when she killed Sarah, she was telling me that my loyalty was secondary to the mission."

Wilfred looked Charlotte in the eye, the desperation of his final, professional play evident. "I stole the money—the twenty million dollars—not to retire, but to lure Petrova to a jurisdiction where she could be identified and legally exposed. The bearer bonds, the transfer lawyer—that was all a trap for Petrova. I knew she would never send a subordinate for that much money. She had to come herself. I needed you, Charlotte. I needed you as the witness to my transfer of the liquidation codes to the D.O.J., knowing that your legal ruthlessness would be the final, perfect defense for my life."

He had been a professional thief, a traitor, and a double agent, all engineered to expose his ultimate controller. His betrayal of the firm had been his final act of vengeance against the woman who had ruined his life.

19:20—The Maintenance Lift

A soft, metallic *shing* echoed from the end of the service corridor. The maintenance lift had arrived.

"Go, Wilfred! Get in the lift!" Charlotte commanded, shoving him toward the opening.

But before Wilfred could move, Dr. Katya Petrova emerged from the smoke-filled utility room, the taser darts discarded, her face a furious mask of hatred. She was moving fast now, abandoning all pretense of judicial authority. She carried the gold-inlaid pistol high, aiming for the flash drive in Charlotte's hand.

"You're not going anywhere, Wilfred!" Petrova screamed, her voice losing its cultured edge. "You were a disposable asset! I should have known your sentimentality would be your weakness!"

Petrova fired two silenced shots, not at Charlotte, but at the control panel of the maintenance lift. The metal sparked, and the lights in the lift flickered and died. The lift was now compromised and locked down.

"Elias! The lift is dead!" Charlotte yelled into the earpiece.

"I know! She blew the primary power conduit! I'm running an emergency override, but it will take sixty seconds to reroute the sub-level energy!" Elias's voice was strained, amplified by the desperate urgency.

Charlotte was trapped. The lift was stalled, the Belgrade operatives were stirring in the living room, and the Kingpin was ten feet away, armed and intent on lethal retrieval.

"You won't defeat me, Ms. Reed," Petrova stated, her eyes gleaming with manic certainty. "I am the financial backbone of the entire political insertion! That drive belongs to me!"

Petrova lunged forward, abandoning the gun to engage Charlotte in hand-to-hand combat—a swift, brutal move that caught Charlotte off guard. Petrova was stronger, more disciplined, and faster than Charlotte had anticipated, years of intelligence training overriding the soft hands of a financial lawyer.

Petrova slammed Charlotte hard against the service corridor wall. The impact knocked the air from Charlotte's lungs, and her grip on the flash drive faltered.

"You think you can fight me? I built the corruption that funded your firm!" Petrova snarled, raising her hand to strike.

Charlotte used the moment of contact to pivot, remembering the training from her brief, high-intensity self-defense course. She brought her elbow up sharply, driving it into Petrova's exposed sternum. Petrova grunted in pain, staggering backward.

Charlotte seized the opportunity. She grabbed the first weapon she could find: a heavy, half-empty can of industrial-grade lubricant oil, left behind by the maintenance crew. She threw the entire contents directly into Petrova's face.

Petrova shrieked, blinded by the sudden, viscous, stinging oil. She stumbled backward, dropping the gold-inlaid pistol onto the polished marble floor of the corridor.

"The gun! Wilfred! Grab the gun!" Charlotte yelled, scrambling for the flash drive which had skittered across the floor.

Wilfred, still disoriented, lunged for the pistol, securing the weapon with trembling hands.

Petrova, blinded, was now struggling to regain her footing, wiping the thick oil from her eyes. She reached desperately for the emergency alarm panel on the wall, intending to bring the entire Monegasque police force down on the penthouse, destroying the codes in the ensuing chaos.

"The alarm! Stop her!" Charlotte screamed, the flash drive now secured in her hand.

Wilfred, clutching the pistol, had the perfect shot. He could eliminate the woman who had ruined his life and murdered his protégée. But the twenty years of professionalism, the years spent orchestrating quiet, financial crimes, prevented him from pulling the trigger. He wasn't a killer.

19:25—The Final Egress

Before Wilfred could make his choice, the main office door, which Lomax Jr. had splintered hours ago, suddenly burst inward again.

It wasn't the police. It was the three Belgrade operatives, having finally recovered from Wilfred's gas attack. They were armed, angry, and fully focused on the retrieval of the liquidation codes. They saw the chaos in the utility room:

Petrova, blinded by oil; Charlotte, unarmed; and Wilfred, holding the gun.

"Codes! Retrieve the codes!" the lead operative yelled, raising his suppressed weapon.

The danger was immediate and absolute. Charlotte knew the operatives would shoot Wilfred first, then her, before securing the codes from her dead body.

Wilfred, realizing the ultimate sacrifice he had to make, threw the gold-inlaid pistol across the floor, sending it skidding toward Petrova.

"Take her, Charlotte! The pistol is out of rounds! Get out!" Wilfred screamed, shoving Charlotte hard toward the now-flickering maintenance lift.

The act was pure misdirection. The Belgrade operatives, seeing the gun being thrown toward their leader, assumed Petrova was the target, and immediately opened fire—not on Wilfred, but on the advancing police force they mistakenly believed was behind Petrova.

The gunfire erupted in a violent, deafening series of bursts, tearing into the walls.

Charlotte didn't hesitate. She grabbed Wilfred and shoved him into the now-reactivated maintenance lift. Elias Vance had succeeded. The emergency power was back.

The last thing Charlotte saw before the doors slammed shut was Petrova recovering her vision, seeing the armed operatives, and realizing the full scale of Wilfred's betrayal. The Kingpin was now trapped between her own killers and the truth.

The lift dropped violently, plunging Charlotte and Wilfred into the darkness of the service shaft. The sounds of the escalating gunfight in the penthouse diminished rapidly above them.

"She's yours, Wilfred," Charlotte gasped, clutching the codes. "She's trapped. The police will find her and the recovered operatives. She's done."

Wilfred leaned against the cold metal wall of the lift, his face pale and etched with exhaustion. "The codes, Charlotte. She has a remote kill-switch tied to the bank accounts. We have maybe four hours before she figures out a way to send the signal to liquidate the funds through a third-party server."

The lift slammed to a smooth stop at the sub-level service tunnel. Elias Vance was waiting, a small, heavily secured briefcase resting on a utility cart.

"We heard the gunshots," Elias said, his eyes wide. "We have sixty seconds before the Monegasque police secure the building. Get in the car."

Charlotte climbed into the armored vehicle Elias had waiting, pulling Wilfred in beside her.

"Where are we going, Elias?" Charlotte demanded, her voice firm, despite the chaos of the last hour. "The D.O.J. is chasing the Covenant List, and the network will assume we're heading back to D.C."

Elias, driving fast through the dark, deserted service tunnels beneath Monte Carlo, looked at her in the rearview mirror. "We can't go to the D.O.J. yet. Petrova is still operational, and she knows the liquidation codes are the only thing that matters. We need a safe harbor with zero surveillance and absolute anonymity—a place where the codes can be secured for a full, verifiable transfer to the international courts."

Wilfred, slumped in the back seat, raised his head, his eyes glinting with the last remnants of his professional cunning. "I know one place. A forgotten, private bank account in a forgotten, remote jurisdiction. The final failsafe. A place

Petrova would never track, because she assumed I wouldn't dare go near the money."

He named the place: a tiny, isolated mountain town in the Swiss Alps, known only for its discreet, ancient banking houses and its absolute neutrality.

"Target: Glarus, Switzerland," Wilfred whispered. "I have a contact there. We secure the codes, and we initiate the final transfer. That is the only place we can ensure the network starves."

Charlotte looked at Elias. "Change of plans. Target: Glarus. The fight for the money—the final weakness—has just begun."

The car screamed out of the tunnel, disappearing onto the dark, winding coastal highway, leaving the glamorous facade of Monaco behind them. The ultimate intelligence war had moved to the high-stakes, anonymous world of Swiss finance.

CHAPTER 18

The Failsafe in the Alps (Charlotte Reed & Wilfred Sinclair)

02:00 (Local Time)—A Private Hangar, Northern Italy

The drive from Monte Carlo to the remote alpine airfield in Northern Italy was a blur of high-speed fear and exhausted silence. The urgency was palpable: Dr. Katya Petrova, the financial architect, was trapped in the penthouse and exposed to Monegasque police, but Wilfred Sinclair had issued a final, chilling warning—she had a remote kill-switch tied to the bank accounts, giving them maybe four hours before she initiated a global liquidation cascade that would vaporize the stolen twenty million dollars.

Elias Vance, driving a high-performance armored vehicle secured from an international contact, maintained a relentless pace through the winding coastal passes. Charlotte Reed sat beside him, the cold steel of the liquidation codes flash drive digging into her palm. In the back seat, Wilfred, recovering from the blast and the shock of his near-fatal confrontation with Petrova, was pale but utterly focused.

"Glarus is the last sanctuary," Wilfred murmured, his voice hoarse from the gas. "It's a micro-jurisdiction. They have banking laws that predate the World Wars. No U.S. warrant, no D.O.J. mandate, and no Interpol request can touch the accounts without a physical, pre-authorized client transfer."

"Which means you are the only one who can move the money," Charlotte concluded, her mind racing, translating the high-stakes game of international intelligence into the cold language of legal contracts and financial mechanisms.

"Not just move it, Charlotte. I have to physically initiate the Final De-liquidation Sequence," Wilfred corrected her. "The money isn't in one account; it's segmented across eight encrypted holding pools. My access code is the only key. Petrova will be scrambling to initiate the override—a coded message sent through a third-party server to the clearing house, instructing them to flag the funds as 'compromised' and 'vaporize' them. We have to beat her to the wire."

They reached the airfield—a small, desolate patch of concrete nestled beneath the imposing, dark mass of the Alps. A single-engine, high-altitude capable jet was waiting on the tarmac, its engines already cycling.

"The flight is thirty minutes to Glarus," Elias said, checking his watch. "That puts us on the ground with maybe three hours to spare before Petrova can recover and initiate the scorched-earth policy."

03:00—Somewhere Over the Swiss Alps

The flight was turbulent, the small jet battling the harsh mountain winds. Charlotte sat opposite Wilfred in the cramped cabin, a small, shielded encryption terminal resting between them. Elias was in the cockpit, maintaining constant, encrypted contact with Anne Austin and Deputy Director Thorne, briefing them on the situation.

Charlotte cut straight to the core of the issue. "Wilfred, I know why you did this. You loved Sarah Jenkins, and Petrova killed her. Your theft was an act of vengeance, designed to expose the network you helped build. But I need to know the final weakness. What did Petrova build into the system that allows her to destroy the money without your codes?"

Wilfred stared at the small, flashing indicator light on the terminal—a light that represented the lifeblood of the Perseus network. "The money was too valuable to ever be seized. I built a system designed to protect the capital from *any* seizure, including a counter-intelligence action. The final layer of security is an automated, self-destruct function tied to a biometric failsafe."

"A biometric failsafe?" Charlotte repeated, her lawyer's skepticism immediately kicking in. "What kind of biometric fail-safe requires physical destruction?"

Wilfred sighed, looking utterly defeated. "It's tied to my personal heart rhythm. I wired the system so that if my heart rate drops below a certain threshold for thirty seconds—indicating death, incapacitation, or extreme duress—the clearing house automatically receives the 'vaporize' command. It's a self-destruct mechanism designed to protect the liquidation codes from torture or coercion. If I am captured, the money dies. If Petrova captures me, she gets the codes, but she loses the money."

Charlotte felt a cold knot tighten in her stomach. "So, if we force you to cooperate and transfer the funds to the D.O.J., and Petrova's remote signal hits the server at the exact moment of transfer, your stress level will peak, triggering the failsafe, and the twenty million vanishes."

"Precisely," Wilfred confirmed, his voice hollow. "The pressure of the moment is the final weakness. It's why I brought us here, Charlotte. We need to find a way to perform the transfer in a state of absolute, clinical calm—a scenario where my biometric signature remains stable, while simultaneously performing the ultimate act of betrayal against the network."

He looked at her, his eyes pleading. "You are the only person who can argue me out of the failsafe, Charlotte. You are the only person who can talk me into betraying my own survival instinct."

04:00—Glarus Banking House, Swiss Alps

The banking house in Glarus was an old, heavy stone structure, nestled between towering peaks, looking more like a monastery than a financial institution. Its security was based on discretion and isolation, not laser grids. The bank vault was deep underground, secured by a massive, centuries-old steel door.

Charlotte, Wilfred, and Elias were met by a single, impeccably dressed bank manager, M. Dubois, who led them through the cold, silent halls to a small, isolated transfer room deep within the vault. The room contained only a single, heavy steel table and a secure terminal linked directly to the international clearing house.

"We have secured the required transfer protocol, M. Sinclair," M. Dubois said, his face stern and neutral. "The transfer of your personal holdings to the specified international non-profit foundation—as per your pre-authorized instructions—can be completed in thirty minutes, provided your identity and the liquidation codes are verified."

Charlotte recognized the setup immediately. Wilfred hadn't planned to save himself; he had planned to donate the money to a non-profit foundation—a legal, irreversible act that would destroy the network's access forever. The donation was the final, devastating move.

Wilfred sat at the terminal, the liquidation codes drive placed beside him. He opened his personal access port, placing his hand over a small, embedded sensor. The system immediately displayed his real-time heart rate and stress indicators. The biometric failsafe was active.

"Elias, run a constant, dedicated scan on all third-party servers linked to Belgrade," Charlotte commanded, pulling up the communication logs. "We need to anticipate the remote kill-switch signal from Petrova. She will use the collapse of the Belgrade network as the trigger."

Elias, setting up his monitoring station across the room, nodded grimly. "I'm running a triple-redundancy scan now. The moment I see the encrypted 'VAPORIZE' command, we have fifteen seconds to abort the transfer or complete it."

The tension in the vault was suffocating. Wilfred placed his hands on the keyboard, his fingers hovering over the complex sequence of codes required for the donation. The transfer was irreversible.

"I can't do it, Charlotte," Wilfred whispered, his heart rate spiking visibly on the small screen. "The fear—the instinct to survive—is overriding the sequence. If I complete the transfer, Petrova will retaliate globally. The fear of that consequence is pushing me into the failsafe zone."

The Legal Failsafe

Charlotte moved, pulling a chair right next to Wilfred, her voice dropping to a low, intense command—the voice she used to break a hostile witness on the stand. This was the most important cross-examination of her career: a cross-examination designed to save her client from his own fear.

"Wilfred, look at me. You are a financial architect. You did not risk everything for survival; you risked everything for revenge and justice for Sarah Jenkins. Don't let Petrova win by using your own fear against you."

"She will find me, Charlotte! She will rebuild the network, and she will find me!"

"No, she won't," Charlotte countered sharply. "Petrova is trapped. The Monegasque police will find the three Belgrade operatives you gassed, they will find the gold-inlaid pistol, and they will link all of it to her flight. The political arm of the network—Fitzgerald, Lomax Jr., the Covenant List—is in D.O.J. custody. Petrova is now a high-profile target of Interpol, flagged for murder and transnational financial fraud. She is running for her life, not rebuilding an empire."

Charlotte leaned in, her gaze relentless. "You are operating on old data, Wilfred. You assume the network is stronger than the law. But the law, backed by the D.O.J., has already cut out the network's political heart. Now we cut out its financial lifeblood. You are not sacrificing your life; you are securing the life of the entire American political system."

She put her hand on his shoulder, the gesture firm and demanding, not comforting. "You have a signed Waiver of Extradition Immunity in your pocket, Wilfred. The D.O.J. will honor it in exchange for the full liquidation of the network. You are not a fugitive; you are an asset who just delivered the greatest blow against foreign espionage in decades. You get your life back, Wilfred. You get your honor back."

Wilfred looked at the screen, his heart rate slowly stabilizing under the weight of her conviction. His financial logic, his professional pride, was battling his terror.

"But the codes, Charlotte," Wilfred whispered. "I can't be responsible for the chaos the network will create when they realize the money is gone."

"Then don't be responsible," Charlotte commanded, her voice rising with finality. "Do your job, Wilfred. Transfer the funds to the non-profit. Let the legal system handle the rest. You are just the architect. Execute the sequence."

Wilfred closed his eyes, took one deep, stabilizing breath, and plunged his fingers onto the keyboard.

He typed the final liquidation codes: a complex, eighteen-digit sequence of numbers and letters. The transfer sequence began, a green bar inching across the screen.

The Final Transfer

04:15—The Glarus Vault

The atmosphere was electric. The transfer was at 50% completion.

Suddenly, Elias Vance slammed his hand onto the table, his eyes fixed on his monitor. "Charlotte! Now! I'm getting a high-frequency ping! Petrova has managed to hijack a remote server in the Indian Ocean! The kill-switch command is initiating! Fifteen seconds to 'vaporize!'"

The emergency override signal was en route. Wilfred's heart rate instantly spiked, the bar on the screen leaping into the red zone—the zone that would trigger the biometric failsafe and destroy the money.

"Wilfred! Don't panic! Complete the sequence!" Charlotte screamed, gripping his shoulder, her eyes fixed on the transfer bar and the heart-rate monitor simultaneously.

The heart-rate monitor was flashing violent, red warnings. Wilfred's hands froze over the keyboard, paralyzed by the overwhelming instinct to survive.

"I can't! The failsafe! It's going to detonate!"

"Look at me, Wilfred! The codes are already transferring! You are safe! You won!" Charlotte yelled, using the final, single piece of legal logic that could override the panic. "You are now D.O.J. Property! You cannot be killed! The deal is done! The money is gone! The network is dead!"

Wilfred's eyes locked onto hers, seeing not the lawyer, but the desperate, winning conviction of the single person who had fought beside him. The legal justification—*D.O.J. Property*—was the only authority he recognized above the network.

He slammed his hand down on the final confirmation key.

The screen flashed TRANSFER 100% COMPLETE.

Wilfred collapsed backward in his chair, gasping, as his heart rate immediately plummeted. The biometric failsafe alarm screamed once, flashing yellow—too late. The money was gone.

Elias confirmed the victory. "Transfer complete! Twenty million dollars successfully routed to the international non-profit foundation. The liquidation codes are archived, and the Perseus funds are zeroed out! Petrova's kill-switch ping arrived three seconds too late!"

Charlotte stared at the empty screen, the finality of the move settling over her. The financial lifeblood of the network was gone.

"The network is starved," Charlotte said, picking up the archived liquidation codes drive and placing it into a secured pouch. "The job is done."

05:00—Glarus Banking House, Swiss Alps

Charlotte and Elias stood on the steps of the ancient banking house. Wilfred Sinclair, pale but stable, stood beside them, no longer a client, not yet a prisoner, but a decisive witness.

Charlotte pulled out her secure phone and dialed Deputy Director Thorne.

"Director Thorne. This is Reed. Phase Two Retrieval is complete. Wilfred Sinclair and the Belgrade funds are secured in Glarus, Switzerland. The entire twenty million dollars has been liquidated and routed to an international, untraceable non-profit foundation. The Perseus network is financially starved, and the liquidation codes are secured."

Thorne's voice, usually reserved, was filled with astonished, grudging admiration. "You did the impossible, Ms. Reed. You won the financial war. We have Fitzgerald and the Covenant List. You have the money and the architect. We will initiate immediate diplomatic seizure of Mr. Sinclair for his testimony."

"I'll be waiting, Director," Charlotte replied, disconnecting the call. She looked at Wilfred, then at the soaring, silent mountains of the Swiss Alps.

"You saved the country, Wilfred," Charlotte admitted, the acknowledgment of his twisted redemption hanging heavy between them.

"I saved myself, Charlotte," Wilfred corrected her, a slow, grim smile returning to his face. "And I left you the final lesson of the game. Never trust the quiet money, and always ensure your defense is absolute."

Charlotte nodded. Her perfect legal record was gone, replaced by a deep knowledge of the intelligence world, a dangerous alliance with a rogue detective, and a partner who was both a traitor and a hero. The murder trial of Senator Gray had ended not in a verdict, but in the collapse of an entire shadow government.

The sun finally crested the sharp mountain peaks, bathing the ancient stone of the bank in a blinding, pure light. Charlotte Reed, the lawyer, was ready to return to Washington D.C. The legal world would never be the same.

CHAPTER 19

The Reckoning (Charlotte Reed & Deputy Director Thorne)

09:30—The Attorney General's Office, Washington D.C.

The contrast between the silent, snow-draped isolation of the Glarus vault and the sterile, humming power of the Attorney General's Executive Suite was stark. Charlotte Reed had traded her armored travel gear for a sharp, impeccably tailored black suit—the uniform of absolute power—but the exhaustion lining her eyes was the mark of the past forty-eight hours. She carried a single, heavily secured briefcase.

She stood across a vast, polished mahogany table from Deputy Director Thorne, who was flanked by three serious, silent men in federal uniform. Thorne's expression was an impossible mix of professional victory and deep personal resentment.

"Ms. Reed, let's be perfectly clear," Thorne began, his voice low and cutting. "We are not here to celebrate. Your partner, Wilfred Sinclair, is currently being held in a secure federal facility and is under three layers of continuous interrogation. He is facing charges of international financial crimes, grand larceny, and conspiracy. He is only protected from immediate federal prosecution by his signed Waiver of Extradition

Immunity, which mandates his full cooperation on the matter of Perseus."

"He is the key witness to the entire financial structure, Director," Charlotte countered, placing the briefcase carefully on the table. "And I risked my life to ensure he was here to testify, something your department failed to do when he was a mere twenty miles from your jurisdiction."

Thorne ignored the jab. "And Detective Anne Austin is currently under investigation by Internal Affairs for destruction of evidence, unlawful search and seizure, and a litany of other charges directly related to the coercion of a federal witness—James Fitzgerald."

Charlotte opened the briefcase. The only items inside were the Liquidation Codes flash drive and the micro SD card containing the Townhome 21 surveillance video.

"The flash drive holds the master archive of the entire Perseus financial ledger. Every transaction, every shell corporation, and every payment made to Senator Gray, Judge Lomax, Sr, and Fitzgerald. That information is worth more than the twenty million dollars Wilfred liquidated. It is the full list of every compromised political asset in the United States," Charlotte stated, pushing the flash drive across the table. "In exchange for that drive, and Wilfred's testimony, you will extend full, irreversible immunity to Detective Anne Austin for all actions taken between the hours of 22:00 on Monday and 03:00 on Wednesday, specifically concerning the retrieval of the Lomax Jr. evidence."

Thorne looked at the flash drive, his expression conflicted. The codes represented a career-defining coup—the dismantling of a major foreign intelligence operation on U.S. soil. But Charlotte's demand represented a major concession to professional criminality.

"Immunity for the lead detective on a murder case who has admitted to breaking the law? That is a non-starter, Ms. Reed. She violated her oath."

"She saved the country from the 21st Juror," Charlotte corrected him, her voice unwavering. "And if you charge her, the entire legal community will know that the D.O.J. prioritized political optics over exposing the most damaging foreign intrusion into the judiciary in history. Your priority is the network, Director, not a reprimand. She is not a criminal; she is an asset who was forced to choose between the rule of law and the fate of the Republic."

She then pushed the micro SD card—the video evidence showing Lomax Jr. staging the murder—across the table.

"This card contains the definitive proof that Joseph Lomax Jr. murdered Sarah Jenkins and then staged the scene to implicate Senator Gray. It also contains the proof that Judge Lomax, Sr, was actively, criminally steering the murder trial to protect his son. With this evidence, the Senator Gray murder charges are dismissed, and your department gains an immediate, ironclad conviction against the actual operative, and the leverage necessary to force a confession from the Judge."

Thorne picked up the SD card, his eyes never leaving Charlotte's face. He knew he was beaten. The immediate political cost of exposing a sitting federal judge as an accessory to murder was astronomical, but the long-term benefit of securing the Perseus ledger was priceless.

Thorne leaned forward, his voice a low hiss. "Immunity is granted to Detective Austin. I will ensure her findings on the Lomax Jr. evidence are credited to a 'special intelligence task force' and that her record remains clean. In return, I want your absolute silence on the involvement of your partner, Wilfred

Sinclair, and your knowledge of the true nature of Senator Gray's political funding."

"Deal," Charlotte affirmed, extending her hand. The exchange was not a handshake of camaraderie, but a cold, necessary transaction between two power players.

11:00—The Dismissal and the Exoneration

Within two hours, the tectonic plates of the U.S. judicial and political landscape shifted violently.

Judge Joseph Lomax, Sr, presiding over a completely different federal case, was quietly and immediately taken into custody by D.O.J. agents on charges related to the obstruction of justice and the conspiracy to aid an international operative. The news was initially couched as a "health emergency" and a "temporary suspension," but the silence from the Supreme Court told the legal community everything they needed to know. The 21st Juror had been removed from the bench.

A new, impartial federal judge was appointed to take over the trial of Senator Marcus David Gray. At the subsequent hearing, Georgia Wright, the Lead Prosecutor, visibly shaken and pale, stood before the new judge. She formally moved to dismiss all charges against Senator Gray, citing "newly discovered, exculpatory evidence" that pointed to a third party.

The murder trial of the century ended not with a bang, but with a weary, anticlimactic legal whimper.

Senator Gray, released from the specter of murder charges, immediately addressed the press, maintaining his innocence and blaming the entire ordeal on a "vicious smear campaign by political rivals." He was free, but Charlotte knew his freedom was temporary. He was politically compromised and now effectively under continuous surveillance by the D.O.J. He was a dead man walking, professionally.

Meanwhile, Detective Anne Austin received the internal memorandum she never thought she would see. Internal Affairs closed her file, and her search of Townhome 21 was credited as a successful "off-book operation" that led to the identification of the true killer, Joseph Lomax Jr. Her reputation was not merely restored; it was elevated.

Anne and Charlotte met later that afternoon in a neutral, quiet cafe near the river—the first time they had spoken outside of a secure line or a life-threatening situation.

"Thorne came through," Anne said quietly, stirring her coffee. "I'm clean. They're giving me a commendation for 'discretion and professional ingenuity.' I don't know whether to laugh or cry."

"Laugh," Charlotte advised, sipping her own espresso. "We leveraged the integrity of the D.O.J. to protect the integrity of your oath. It's the ultimate legal paradox."

"And Wilfred Sinclair?"

"He is singing in federal custody. They have confirmed everything: the money laundering, the recruitment of Sarah Jenkins, the staged murder. His testimony, combined with the ledger, will lead to dozens of arrests across the State Department, finance, and intelligence. He bought his freedom, Anne, at the cost of everything he had. That's a verdict I can live with."

Anne looked at Charlotte, admiration and caution mingling in her gaze. "And what about you, Charlotte Reed? You suborned a federal investigation, you coerced a witness, you obstructed justice, and you used information from a known intelligence agent to win a political war. Your perfect record is intact, but the ethics board would have your license for lunch."

Charlotte gave a tired, knowing smile. "I won the war, Anne. But I resigned from the firm three hours ago. I'm taking an indefinite leave of absence. My life is now a high-value target for any remaining Perseus elements, and my ethical foundation has been rebuilt with a new, more pragmatic definition of justice. I cannot go back to arguing corporate espionage cases."

Anne nodded, understanding the professional and personal toll the case had taken. "What's next, then?"

Charlotte looked toward the Capitol building, barely visible through the window. "The real work, Detective. Senator Gray is acquitted of murder, but he is a foreign asset. The D.O.J. can only observe him. I need to know the final truth of his complicity. Did he knowingly participate in the treason, or was he just the unwitting, magnetic face of the operation? That answer determines his final fate."

14:30—Senator Gray's Temporary Office, Capitol Hill

Charlotte went to see Senator Marcus David Gray for the last time. The Senator sat behind his massive desk, bathed in the celebratory light of his dismissal. He looked less stressed, but more empty. The political machinery had saved him, but the man had been hollowed out.

"Charlotte, come in! A bottle of the finest champagne is chilling! We did it! They folded!" Gray crowed, gesturing toward the dismissal notice. "I knew the evidence was flimsy. I knew the truth would prevail."

Charlotte remained standing, her expression serious. "The truth, Senator, is that you are acquitted of murder because we proved someone else killed Sarah Jenkins. The truth is that you were the central target of a foreign intelligence operation known as Perseus, designed to install you as the President of the United States."

Gray's smile evaporated. His eyes darted nervously to the secure communications terminal on his desk.

"That is an absurd, paranoid fantasy, Charlotte. You sound like Wilfred Sinclair."

"Wilfred Sinclair confirmed that your campaign was funded by Dr. Katya Petrova's shell corporations. The liquidation codes proved that every dollar spent on your rise to power—from the earliest primaries to the murder victim's salary—was laundered through Belgrade. You didn't win your acquittal, Senator. The D.O.J. used you as bait to secure the greater ledger."

Charlotte laid her final card on the table, not for a verdict, but for her own closure. "I need to know one thing, Senator. Was this entirely about the money and the political leverage, or did you know you were the designated Foreign Asset? Were you knowingly committing treason against the nation you vowed to lead?"

Gray stared at his hands for a long moment, the practiced charisma replaced by sheer, raw terror. He finally looked up, his eyes meeting hers, and the answer was a horrifying, quiet confession.

"When Sarah was killed, I was terrified," Gray whispered, the voice of the presidential hopeful replaced by the voice of a broken puppet. "But before that... yes. I knew. I was not recruited for my ideology, Charlotte. I was recruited for my weakness, for my debt, and for my ambition. Petrova and Wilfred brought me in over a decade ago. They groomed me, they guided me, and they silenced every obstacle. I am a foreign asset, Charlotte. But I am an *American* asset now. I was just trying to do the country a favor, clean up the rot, and stop the petty infighting."

Charlotte felt a surge of cold fury. Gray had committed the ultimate, quiet betrayal, not for profit, but for power.

"You didn't do the country a favor, Senator," Charlotte said, picking up her briefcase. "You almost handed the keys to the kingdom to a hostile power, and you let a good woman die in the process. You are free of the murder charge, but you will never be free of the surveillance, the debt, or the treason. You can't save the country from the outside, Senator. You have to fight for it from the inside, and you chose the wrong side."

She turned and walked to the door.

"Where are you going, Charlotte?" Gray pleaded, his voice cracking. "I need counsel! I need protection! They will still come for me!"

Charlotte paused at the threshold. "You are no longer my client, Senator. And the only protection you have now is the protection I negotiated for the D.O.J.'s surveillance team. Enjoy the rest of your term."

17:00—The Final Judgment (Charlotte Reed & Judge Joseph Lomax, Sr.)

Charlotte was granted an interview room at the D.O.J.'s secured facility—a meeting with the final, tragic figure of the conspiracy: Judge Joseph Lomax, Sr.

The Judge was a diminished figure, seated across the steel table, wearing a beige prison jumpsuit. His authority was gone, replaced by the crushing weight of his compromise.

"They offered me a plea deal, Charlotte," the Judge said, his voice flat. "Testify against my son, Joseph Jr., and Petrova, and I get leniency. I save the integrity of the bench from further public humiliation. They want me to wear a wire."

"And what is your choice, Judge?" Charlotte asked, her voice professional, stripped of any emotion.

"My choice was made five years ago, when I paid half a million dollars to silence the fraud charges against my boy," the Judge admitted, looking Charlotte straight in the eye. "I chose my son over my oath. I chose him again when Petrova and Fitzgerald came to me and told me he had done the unthinkable—that he had killed the girl and framed the Senator. They told me if I didn't steer the case, my son would face the death penalty. I protected him, Charlotte. I chose fatherhood over the law. I am the 21st Juror because I was the single person who allowed an unjust verdict to prevail."

"You didn't just choose your son, Judge," Charlotte corrected him gently, placing the liquidation codes drive on the table between them. "You chose a foreign power over the Constitution. Petrova leveraged your paternal weakness to compromise the highest levels of American justice. Your son is a trained operative, Judge. He used you. He used your weakness to protect the network."

The Judge stared at the drive, the full weight of the global conspiracy crashing down on him.

"Is my son safe?" he asked, the question agonizingly small.

"Your son is in federal custody, and he will face charges for murder and espionage," Charlotte confirmed. "But he is alive, Judge. His life was the price of the mission. Now, you have one final choice: Protect the memory of the Judge you were meant to be, or protect the son who used you for treason. You can deliver the final, devastating testimony against Petrova and your son, or you can let the record show that the 21st Juror sold his country for a lie."

The Judge slumped forward, his hands covering his face. The long, agonizing silence in the interview room was the final, unspoken verdict.

"Tell Thorne I'll testify," Judge Lomax, Sr. finally whispered. "I will tell them everything. But I want full assurance that my son gets a fair trial, and that my story is erased from the court's official record. I want to save the integrity of the bench, even if I destroy myself."

Charlotte nodded. She had won the final piece of the puzzle. The financial collapse, the political humiliation, and the judicial corruption—all traced back to the single, tragic figure of the compromised father.

She stood to leave, pausing at the door. "You made the right choice, Judge. The true verdict is not rendered by the jury. It's rendered by history."

Charlotte left the secured facility, walking out into the late afternoon sun. The case was closed. The Senator was free but watched, the Detective was exonerated, the financial architect was exposed, and the Judge had found his final, agonizing redemption. Her perfect record was intact, but her life as a defense attorney was over. The game had changed forever.

CHAPTER 20

The Treason Tribunal (Charlotte Reed)

10:00—Defense Command Center (Secured Annex), Washington D.C.

Charlotte Reed stepped back into the sterile, forgotten conference room in the federal annex, the air thick with the faint, lingering scent of burnt sulfur and fear—a perfect metaphor for the state of the capital. She was no longer wearing the black suit of a power attorney, but the functional, travel-worn clothes of someone who had just finished a transnational intelligence war.

The room was operational once more, controlled not by her paralegal team, but by the watchful presence of Deputy Director Samuel Thorne of the D.O.J. Counter-Intelligence Division and two grim-faced federal agents. The long mahogany table was covered not with legal pads, but with secured satellite equipment and the now-infamous titanium case that held the Covenant List and the archived liquidation codes from Glarus.

Thorne rose, his gaze sharp and assessing. He offered no handshake, only a curt nod of professional acknowledgment. "Ms. Reed. Welcome back to the theatre of operations. Your flight from Switzerland confirms the transfer of the Perseus funds was successful. You and Mr. Vance delivered what Interpol could not."

"The funds are gone, Director Thorne," Charlotte stated, placing the final, titanium-sealed drive containing the Glarus codes onto the table. "Twenty million dollars are liquidated to an international non-profit, and the Perseus network is financially dead. Wilfred Sinclair is in the custody of Swiss authorities, pending immediate diplomatic transfer to the D.O.J. He will cooperate fully under the terms of his immunity agreement."

"And Dr. Katya Petrova?" Thorne pressed.

"The Monegasque police secured Petrova after the failed assassination attempt in the Tour Odéon penthouse. She is facing charges related to the local gunfight, and Interpol is already working on extradition for the conspiracy. The Kingpin is neutralized," Charlotte confirmed, her voice ringing with finality.

The Washington phase of the conflict was now over. The time for maneuvering was past; the time for the reckoning had arrived.

"Then the time for secrecy is over," Thorne said, his voice dropping to a low, intense register. "The Covenant List is decrypted. It is far worse than we anticipated, Ms. Reed. Six sitting U.S. Senators, the former Attorney General, three campaign committee chairs—all on the Belgrade payroll for years. The evidence you provided has compromised the entire D.C. structure. We cannot prosecute this politically; we must prosecute this under the umbrella of National Security. The murder of Sarah Jenkins will be the vehicle for the exposure of wholesale treason."

The Political Earthquake

11:30—Attorney General's Office, Washington D.C.

Within the hour, the Attorney General's office released a series of simultaneous, devastating statements that shook the U.S. political foundation to its core.

The first statement announced the immediate and unconditional dismissal of all murder charges against Senator Marcus David Gray. The D.O.J. cited "newly acquired, conclusive forensic and testimonial evidence" that definitively identified the killer as Joseph Lomax Jr. and confirmed the staged nature of the crime scene. The entire world media, which had been tracking the case for weeks, erupted. The President's favorite candidate was cleared of murder, but the story was only just beginning.

The second statement announced the immediate federal arrest and indictment of Judge Joseph Lomax, Sr. on charges of obstruction of justice, conspiracy to aid a foreign operative, and, most damningly, treason. The D.O.J. confirmed that the Judge had been compromised by the foreign-funded network, Perseus, to protect his son and steer the Senator Gray murder trial. The 21st Juror was exposed, and the entire judicial structure was reeling from the internal betrayal.

The third, most explosive statement was the indictment of James Fitzgerald, Senator Gray's longtime personal aide, on multiple counts of espionage and treason. The D.O.J. confirmed that Fitzgerald, the alleged "Gatekeeper" of the network, had orchestrated the payment of foreign funds to compromise U.S. politicians.

The final, decisive blow came in the form of a controlled, anonymous leak to the *Washington Post*—a partial, heavily redacted list of the political figures named on the Covenant List.

It was enough. Six Senators, including two committee chairmen who had been fixtures of the Intelligence community for decades, were immediately named as recipients of untraceable funds tied to the Belgrade network. The political landscape of D.C. didn't just shift; it shattered. Impeachments, resignations, and mass resignations followed in a rapid, self-preserving cascade.

The Final Verdicts

15:00—Federal D.O.J. Annex, Secured Interrogation Room

Charlotte Reed was allowed a final, private meeting with Detective Anne Austin, who had spent the day sequestered in a secure safe house, watching the legal victories unfold on the news. Anne's arm was still in a cast, but the weariness had been replaced by fierce vindication.

"Thorne came through," Anne said, looking at the news feed showing a distraught Senator Gray addressing the press. "My record is clean. My findings on Townhome 21 are now the foundation of a federal treason inquiry. We didn't just solve a murder, Charlotte; we saved the next election."

"We made Thorne look like a hero, which was the final condition of the deal," Charlotte observed, allowing herself a small, tired smile. "Gray is acquitted of murder, but his political career is over. He is now the most watched man in America—a compromised asset who is no longer useful to anyone."

Joseph Lomax Jr., the killer, was the next piece of the reckoning. Thorne granted him immunity from the murder charge—the promise Charlotte had made—in exchange for his full cooperation against the network's remaining assets and the final decryption of the Belgrade systems. The D.O.J. had traded one life for the dismantling of an entire foreign operation.

Judge Joseph Lomax, Sr, the tragic figure, was the final verdict. He agreed to testify against his son and the network in exchange for a limited, supervised release—a fate that was a judicial death sentence but a reprieve from prison. He would live out his days in quiet shame, the 21st Juror silenced forever.

The Ultimate Trade (Charlotte Reed & Wilfred Sinclair)

17:00—JFK International Airport, New York

Charlotte stood on the tarmac of a secure, private hangar, waiting for the arrival of the small Gulfstream carrying Wilfred Sinclair and the diplomatic escort from Switzerland. The Swiss had released Wilfred into U.S. federal custody, recognizing the political necessity of the handover.

Wilfred emerged from the plane, looking tired but utterly composed, dressed in a standard, unadorned suit. He had survived the collapse of his financial empire, the assassination attempt, and the legal fallout. He was no longer Charlotte's partner, nor her client, but the key to her final freedom.

Thorne was there, supervising the transfer. "Mr. Sinclair, you are in federal custody. The immunity deal stands only for your financial crimes and your involvement with Perseus. Any attempt to flee or mislead the investigation will result in immediate prosecution for grand larceny and obstruction."

Wilfred ignored Thorne, his eyes fixed on Charlotte. "I kept my end of the bargain, Charlotte. I delivered the money, and I delivered the codes. The network is finished."

"You delivered the network, Wilfred, but you also stole twenty million dollars of operating capital and nearly killed me in the process," Charlotte reminded him, her voice low. "You played the long con, and you used me as your shield. You risked my integrity and my life."

Wilfred accepted the accusation with a slight nod. "My life for your perfect record, Charlotte. It was always an equitable transaction. I knew you would survive because I knew your ambition was greater than my fear."

Charlotte pulled a manila envelope from her briefcase. It contained her final legal move—the one that would seal the deal and settle the moral score.

"The D.O.J. immunity deal guarantees your life, Wilfred. But I know you. You can't live without structure. You can't live without the game."

She handed him the envelope. Inside was a single, laminated document: a Consultancy Contract for a new, private, international foundation—the very non-profit organization into which the twenty million dollars had been routed in Glarus.

"The non-profit needs a brilliant financial mind to manage the twenty million dollars and ensure the funds are used to track and fight future transnational political corruption," Charlotte explained. "The money is clean. The job is legal. You manage the money and you run the counter-intelligence finances for the foundation. You work for me, Wilfred. And you spend the rest of your life cleaning up the wreckage you helped create."

Wilfred stared at the contract, his eyes wide with surprise, then slowly, a deep, genuine smile spread across his face—the look of a man who had not just survived, but had been given a new, impossible game to master.

"You won, Charlotte," Wilfred said, his voice imbued with respect. "The ultimate legal coup. You traded my freedom for my servitude. I accept the contract."

The New Mandate (Charlotte Reed & Deputy Director Thorne)

Thorne watched the exchange with thinly veiled shock. "You're hiring a witness to a federal crime, Ms. Reed? And giving him control of the money he stole?"

"I'm ensuring that the twenty million dollars that was designed to destroy the country is now used to save it, Director Thorne," Charlotte countered, closing the briefcase. "The D.O.J. is great at prosecution, but terrible at long-term prevention. That is my new mandate."

Charlotte walked over to Thorne, delivering her final, personal closing argument.

"I have resigned from the law firm. My record is intact, but my understanding of justice is fundamentally changed. I can no longer sit in a courtroom and argue corporate espionage cases, knowing what I know about the true levers of power."

She looked toward the city skyline, where the political machinery was currently tearing itself apart under the weight of the Covenant List.

"The treason is exposed, but the global threat remains. There will be another Perseus network, another compromised Judge, and another puppet Asset. I am going to find them, Director Thorne, long before they reach the D.C. courtroom."

Thorne, recognizing the transformation in the woman before him—the lawyer who had become an intelligence operative—nodded slowly. "And what about Detective Anne Austin? What is her final verdict?"

"Detective Austin is being promoted to the FBI's newly created Judicial Integrity Task Force," Charlotte announced, her pride evident. "She is the one honest cop who survived the corruption, and she will be spending the rest of her career ensuring the Bench remains clean."

Charlotte extended her hand to Thorne, this time for a farewell, not a transaction. "The case is closed, Director. But the war has just begun."

Thorne took her hand, the contact firm and cold. "Be careful, Ms. Reed. The people you hunt do not respect the rule of law, or the rules of engagement."

Charlotte smiled, the look a blend of exhaustion, certainty, and dangerous anticipation.

"I stopped respecting the rules the moment I realized the Bench was compromised, Director. And I stopped being a mere lawyer the moment the 21st Juror was revealed."

She turned and walked across the tarmac toward a waiting car, leaving the legal world, the chaos, and the compromised city behind her. Her new life had begun—a life spent in the shadows, fighting the enemies of the state, armed with nothing but her intelligence, her tenacity, and the dangerous truth she now possessed. The 21st Juror had been found, but the work of justice was truly just beginning. The end of the trial was merely the beginning of the hunt.

The End

SNEAK PEEK: THE FINAL BROKER

(A New Thriller by Frederick Campbell)

04:00—Istanbul

Charlotte Reed was not in the mood for Turkish coffee. Or political negotiations.

Exactly six months had passed since she traded her perfect legal record for an unlimited mandate to hunt down the remnants of the **Perseus** network. Her life was now a string of secure drops, encrypted burner phones, and the cold, unyielding knowledge that the entire U.S. government owed her a debt it couldn't pay.

Her current target, a man known only as 'The Broker,' was the highest-ranking Perseus operative still at large. He was responsible for placing the very individuals who signed off on Judge Lomax's black ops budget.

The Broker had just secured a highly sensitive shipment: the final, original, pre-war manifest of **Wilfred Sinclair's** financial accounts—a document that proved not only Wilfred's crimes but implicated dozens of powerful entities in London and Geneva who thought they were safe.

A message from Wilfred, now running Charlotte's counter-finance foundation from Glarus, flashed on her secure wrist terminal: *He's moving the Manifest to Zurich by dawn. If he gets it to the Clearing House, we lose the last piece of leverage on the Western European assets. Stop him, Charlotte. By any means necessary.*

Charlotte looked across the darkened bazaar toward the Turkish Intelligence officer guarding the Broker's exit route. The man had a clear, professional demeanor, but his eyes held the familiar, empty glint of a compromised asset.

She drew the silenced P30 from her coat. Her mission was to retrieve the manifest, not eliminate the Broker. But as always, the rules of engagement had just been rewritten.

The Broker walked out, clutching a thin, leather-bound portfolio.

Charlotte stepped into the light, leaving the comfort of the shadows behind.

The war for the rule of law was not over. It had simply gone global.

ACKNOWLEDGMENTS

No book is written in isolation, especially one that requires the intricate weaving of legal, financial, and intelligence narratives. My deepest gratitude goes to the analysts who provided insight into the mechanisms of international financial crimes, particularly in jurisdictions like Monaco and Glarus. Your expertise helped craft the framework of the **Perseus** network and gave credibility to Wilfred Sinclair's final maneuvers.

To my colleagues, collaborators, and early readers: your relentless demand for pace and clarity pushed this story forward. I am forever grateful for your uncompromising editorial eye.

And finally, to the reader: thank you for believing in the truth that hides beneath the official record. I hope to see you on the next battlefield.

AUTHOR'S NOTE

While *The 21st Juror* is a work of pure fiction, it delves into the very real challenges facing the integrity of our judiciary and political systems. The notion that an elected official or a judge could be compromised by transnational influence—a subtle, calculated process spanning decades rather than a single event—is a constant pressure point in modern democracy.

The legal concepts of **ex parte communication, judicial recusal,** and the use of financial vehicles like **shell corporations** are all drawn from reality, even if the extreme circumstances presented here are entirely imagined.

The character of **Charlotte Reed** is driven by a question I've always found compelling: **What is the breaking point where legal ethics must yield to moral necessity?** When the law itself is used as a weapon against the state, the traditional line between defense attorney and intelligence operative blurs.

Thank you for joining Charlotte on this high-stakes journey. I hope the adrenaline rush of this investigation stays with you long after the final page.

— Frederick Campbell

ABOUT THE PUBLISHER

MK Storyworks is a truly global book publisher, dedicated to the timeless mission of connecting compelling authors with enthusiastic readers across the world.

We pride ourselves on curating a diverse and dynamic list that spans the full spectrum of literary interests. Whether you are looking for an immersive escape into a bestselling fiction novel, seeking wisdom and knowledge from groundbreaking non-fiction titles, perfecting a dish with our acclaimed cookbooks, or introducing the magic of reading to the next generation with our enchanting children's books, MK Storyworks delivers stories that inform, entertain, and inspire.

Our commitment to quality, creativity, and global reach ensures that every book we publish finds its place in the hands and hearts of readers, no matter where they are.

Connect with MK Storyworks

Stay up-to-date with our latest releases, author news, and behind-the-scenes glimpses by connecting with us online:

Website: www.mkstoryworks.com

www.ingramcontent.com/pod-product-compliance
Lightning Source LLC
Chambersburg PA
CBHW031239210726
48287CB00003B/830